"It was pretty hectic," Fausto said

Tanya listened at dinner as he described his plans to transfer his business interests to Milan.

Her eyes kept hypnotically drifting to the oddly sensuous movement of his lips. What was the matter with her? "By the way," she said, "your friend, the countess, telephoned."

"Bea?" The dark brows lifted. "I hope you were polite to her."

Tanya stiffened. "Is it important whether I was polite or not?"

He looked at her for a long hard moment. "Yes, Tanya, it is. Bea is a friend as well as a client, and I expect you to treat her with civility."

"I don't need lectures on how to conduct myself—whether it's with your clients or your mistress," she stormed. "I'm aware of my inferior position here."

"Good," he said, his lips a thin white line. "At least you've got one thing straight."

STEPHANIE HOWARD is a British author whose two amibitions since childhood were to see the world and write. Her first venture into the world was a four-year stay in Italy, learning the language, and supporting herself by writing short stories. Then her sensible side brought her back to London to read Social Administrations at the London School of Economics. She has held various editorial posts at magazines such as *Reader's Digest*, *Vanity Fair*, *Women's Own*, as well as writing free-lance for *Cosmopolitan*, *Good Housekeeping* and *The Observer*. However, she has spent the past six years happily trotting around the globe. Last year she returned to the U.K. to write. She hopes this first book in the Harlequin Presents line will be followed by many others.

STEPHANIE HOWARD

reluctant prisoner

Harlequin Books

TORONTO • NEW YORK • LONDON
AMSTERDAM • PARIS • SYDNEY • HAMBURG
STOCKHOLM • ATHENS • TOKYO • MILAN

Harlequin Presents first edition August 1988
ISBN 0-373-11098-7

Original hardcover edition published in 1987
by Mills & Boon Limited

Printed in U.S.A.

CHAPTER ONE

FROM the top of the hill, Tanya had a perfect view of the house and the road. She smiled to herself. It was an ideal vantage point. She sank down on the warm grass, slightly out of breath after her long climb. Here she could watch unobserved for them to arrive, then go back down and make her entrance when they least expected it.

Her mouth twisted doubtfully at the thought. The ploy might give her some brief psychological advantage in the uneasy confrontation that lay ahead, but it was hardly likely to change the inevitable, humiliating outcome of things. At this point, nothing could do that.

A soft breeze stirred the mass of golden curls that framed her face, and the early morning sun reflected sharply in the tawny eyes as Tanya laid her chin against her knees and hugged her slim legs to her chest. She felt a hot stab of regret as she gazed down at the scene below. It was hard to accept that all of this was on the point of being lost. The seventeenth-century, half-timbered house that she had loved and lived in all her life, the surrounding acre of garden set amid the softly rolling Sussex hills—and, above all, the happy, carefree way of life that she had once known in this place. All now sadly part of the past. Or very soon about to be.

She shrugged and fixed her eyes determinedly on the road below. No point in dwelling on all that now. Any minute, they would be here—Renata and the man who held her father's future in his hands. And not only the future of her father, Tanya acknowledged with a bitter smile. To some extent, this stranger held her own fate in balance, too.

With a shiver, she tugged the hem of her light wool dress over her knees. It could have been worse, she reminded herself impatiently. Much worse. Less than forty-eight hours ago, the future had seemed too bleak even to contemplate.

Renata's unexpected phone call from Rome the evening before last had changed all that. '*Cara!*' The rich, warm tones of her old friend had instantly lifted Tanya's spirits a notch. Renata was always so positive, so practical. This time, though, she had simply sounded concerned. 'I've just heard the terrible news about your father—about his heart attack, about the terrible state his business is in. *Cara* Tanya——' there had been a note of gentle chiding in the older woman's voice '—why didn't you phone to let me know immediately? If I didn't love you both so much, I'd be very cross indeed with you.'

Tanya had felt a foolish lump rise in her throat. Dear Renata. She was probably one of the few who really did care. 'I'm sorry,' she had answered, trying to disguise the sudden catch in her voice, 'but things have been so hectic lately, I've never really had a chance——' Her voice trailed off. If only Renata knew what a nightmare the whole ghastly business had been.

'Of course, poor child. I understand.' The older woman's warmth reached out to comfort her. 'But, tell me, how is your father now?'

Tanya had taken a deep breath as she had thought of the pale, sad figure in the bed upstairs. The once proud and successful Devlin Sinclair, fine art dealer and worldly connoisseur, had aged almost unrecognisably over the past two years. The death of his wife, the collapse of his business and now this sudden heart attack had reduced him to a spectre of his former self. Deep furrows had gouged themselves around the wide, once-humorous mouth, and the bright, intelligent eyes were sunken and lifeless now.

'Not good,' she answered, seeing no point in keeping the cruel truth from her friend. 'He's improving, but too slowly, the doctors say.' And then she had forced herself to speak out loud the words that scared her just to think of them. 'The trouble is, Renata, he doesn't seem to care any more whether he gets well again or not.' It sounded melodramatic, but it was true, and she added, 'I hate to say this, but I think my father's lost his will to live.'

There had been a long, poignant silence at the other end. Then, 'What about his business? Will he be able to save it?' Renata had wanted to know.

'Oh, there's no hope of that.' Hopeless tears welled in her eyes. She had been struggling with the wretched situation on her own for so long now it was hardly surprising if the strain was finally starting to tell on her. 'The business is finished,' she managed to blurt out miserably. 'We expect it to be put into the hands of the Official Receiver by the end of the month.'

'What?' Renata had sounded horrified. 'You mean that Devlin is to be declared bankrupt? But we can't allow this to happen, *cara* Tanya. Why, a proud man like your father—the shame of it would kill him!'

Precisely the fear that preyed relentlessly on Tanya's mind. 'But there's nothing to be done. I've discussed the whole thing endlessly with my father's solicitors.'

'*Cara*, there is always *something* that can be done.' A short pause as Renata hastily gathered her thoughts. 'Give me twenty-four hours. I'll phone again tomorrow at the same time. Give my love to Devlin—and cheer up. If there's a way, we'll find it, I promise you.'

The next twenty-four hours had been the longest that

Tanya had ever endured. It had seemed fanciful and foolish to believe that Renata could do anything to save the situation now, but she was their last hope—and Tanya had clung to that hope with a kind of desperate optimism. Besides, she had felt intuitively that Renata would not let her father down.

Renata Cabrini had swept into the Sinclairs' lives about four years ago. Devlin's name had been recommended to her by some mutual acquaintance in New York, and she had come to him looking for some nineteenth-century English watercolours for her new Manhattan apartment. Tanya, who had been working for her father's Sussex-based business at the time, had taken to the elegant, flamboyant and thoroughly warm-hearted woman instantly. A friendship had developed, and over the years Tanya had come to admire as well as love Renata for the remarkable, indomitable individual that she was. Now she was about to discover just how resourceful, and caring, her friend could be.

The phone call the following evening had been brief and to the point. 'I'm coming over on the first flight tomorrow,' Renata had announced. 'And I'm bringing Fausto with me.'

'Fausto?'

'My brother, *cara* Tanya. He's the financial wizard in our family, and he already has a plan sketched out. He'll want to see your father's lawyers, so make an appointment for some time in the afternoon. And tell them to have all the facts and figures available. Fausto will want to study them. OK, I'll see you tomorrow, *cara*,' Renata had finished, without giving Tanya the opportunity to say a word. '*Ciao*—and sleep well. Your worries are over.'

The news, for some reason, had disturbed Tanya more than it had set her mind at rest. And though she knew that it was totally illogical, she somehow couldn't quell the strange disquiet that she felt. Fausto Cabrini was no more than a name to her, a shadowy figure in the background of Renata's life. Tanya knew little about him beyond the fact that he had inherited a few years previously, on his father's death, the vastly wealthy Cabrini industrial empire, and that he was in addition a highly successful investment consultant in his own right. A complex, powerful and ambitious man, by all accounts—with more than a passing reputation for ruthlessness—it seemed he was about to step out of the shadows and into the very centre of her life. And already she knew, without knowing why, that she bitterly resented him.

She straightened abruptly as a taxi cab came into view, moving swiftly, heading for the house. And she scrambled quickly to her feet and nervously brushed a strand of gold hair from her face. It must be them. She held her breath as the black cab disappeared behind a clump of trees and admonished herself silently for being so negative. Fausto Cabrini was her father's only hope. If he was unable to offer help, Devlin was lost. And she sighed with relief as the cab came into view again. She owed this man her gratitude, not her dislike. Besides, it was ridiculous. She hadn't even met him yet!

As the cab left the road and swept up the narrow drive to the front of the house, Tanya felt her fists clench at her sides. So much depended on this meeting with Renata's brother. For her father's sake, she must be nice to him—even woo him a little if that would help. And she frowned and peered down as the cab came to a halt. What was he like anyway, this Fausto Cabrini?

Almost simultaneously the rear doors of the cab swung open and two figures emerged. One, an elegant woman in red—Renata—the other, a man in a slim, dark suit. But Tanya managed to catch no more than a fleeting, tantalising glimpse, and she was too far away to see clearly anyway. The next instant the man was striding briskly towards the front door of the house—with Renata hurrying at his heels. A moment later they were both inside.

Tanya brushed the dry grass from her dress and started slowly down the hill. By the time she got back to the house they would be waiting in her father's study where Devlin had insisted on receiving them. She forced her features into a determinedly enthusiastic smile as she picked her way through the long, blown grass. Then she would make her entrance.

'Tanya! How wonderful to see you! You're looking well.' Renata came hurrying up to greet her the moment she walked through the study door and kissed her warmly on both cheeks. 'We were just asking Devlin where you were.'

Tanya threw her father a reassuring smile. He was seated behind his desk, a thin, frail figure—though he had made an effort to look his most businesslike today, his grey hair sleek, the smart suit lending him an air of fragile authority. 'I went for a walk,' she offered to the room at large. 'I hope I didn't hold you up.'

'Not at all, *signorina*. We took the liberty of starting without you.' The dark-suited figure seated opposite her father at the desk spoke without even bothering to glance up at her. A rasp of impatience sounded in the smooth, deep voice. 'My appointment with your father was for nine o'clock, I understand. It is now almost thirteen minutes past.'

Tanya felt as though she had been slapped. So much for her grand entrance! Her feeble effort to maintain some measure of control over the situation had very

evidently backfired. And her eyes narrowed warily as
Fausto Cabrini laid down the sheaf of papers he had been
studying and with mock politeness rose to his feet.

He was a tall man, with the same dark good looks as his
sister—though the finely chiselled nose, square jaw and
strong, athletic build were wholly, aggressively masculine. And he had about him what Tanya could only
describe to herself later as an aura of barely restrained
animal power. This man, she sensed at once, was
dangerous. As he turned at last to look at her—and
smiled with that special brand of poise that only the very
privileged possess—she felt her hackles rise instinctively.
It had been on the tip of her tongue to offer some
apology for her lateness, but perversely now she bit it
back. She would apologise to this man for nothing.

Renata was standing between them. 'Let me introduce you to Tanya,' she intervened quickly, 'Devlin's
daughter. Tanya, this is my brother Fausto.'

Dark, almost black eyes swept over her, taking in at
one practised glance the mane of bright gold hair, clear,
creamy skin and the almost voluptuous curve of her
breasts above the tiny, cinched-in waist and shapely
hips. Tanya felt herself flush indignantly. She was
wearing a high-necked, long-sleeved woollen dress, yet
he had looked at her as though she were standing there
naked. Cool, strong fingers clasped hers momentarily.
'Glad you could make it *signorina*. So good of you in the
circumstances to spare a few minutes of your precious
time.' The sarcasm in his voice was almost tangible.

'No trouble, Signor Cabrini. No trouble at all,' she
countered with a stiff, false smile. Her earlier resolution
to be nice to him was going to prove more than a little
difficult to fulfil. Wooing him was out of the question.
For one thing, it would be a total waste of time, she
sensed. Even if she had the stomach to try.

'Good.' He lifted one eyebrow in a mocking indict-
ment, and his eyes held hers for a moment longer before
he turned abruptly to address her father. 'Now that the
introductions are over, Mr Sinclair, I suggest that we
get down to business properly. We have a great deal of
ground to cover and comparatively little time.' He cast a
cursory glance towards Renata and Tanya. 'Perhaps the
ladies would like to leave us now?'

If Tanya's cheeks were flushed before, they blazed
with indignation now. 'If you don't mind, Signor
Cabrini, this particular lady has not the slightest
intention of meekly leaving the room while the grown-
ups get down to discussing business. I want to hear every
single word of your proposal.' Her eyes stared levelly
into his. 'And besides, I'm sure that my father would
prefer me to stay.'

He regarded her in cool silence for a minute and she
fancied she saw a flash of anger illuminate the deep, dark
eyes. Fausto Cabrini was clearly unaccustomed to
having his pronouncements questioned, Tanya sensed,
and particularly not by members of the female sex. Then
the well shaped mouth seemed to quirk at one corner in a
fleeting and totally derisive smile as he inclined his head
in Devlin's direction again. 'Is that what you wish, Mr
Sinclair? That your daughter be present at our
discussion?'

Devlin nodded. He had been quiet so far, apparently
overwhelmed by the unexpected direction that events
had suddenly started moving in, but his voice was firm
and steady when he spoke. 'Yes, if you don't mind,
Signor Cabrini, I'd prefer Tanya to stay. Whatever
transpires is going to affect her life as well as mine. She
has a right to be in on it.'

Fausto Cabrini turned to Tanya with an acid smile.
'You are permitted to stay with the grown-ups after all,'

he purred, but softly, so that only she could hear. Then he added more loudly, as he indicated one of the button-backed chairs that stood around her father's desk, 'I suggest you sit here, next to me, *signorina*. That way you will miss nothing. And please feel free to take notes if you wish.'

She ignored the mocking amusement in his voice. 'I may well do that,' she retorted archly, deliberately shifting her chair a couple of feet away from his as she sat down. 'I always think it's wise to keep records—in the interests of all parties concerned.'

He caught her gibe neatly and threw it back at her. 'Don't worry, *signorina*,' he murmured, eyeing her dispassionately. 'Any agreement that your father and I may come to will be drawn up jointly by his lawyers and mine—and I shall see to it personally that you are provided with a copy for your own private scrutiny. With explanatory notes, of course.'

Tanya could do very little but seethe inwardly as Renata slipped off discreetly to make coffee and her brother launched into a remarkably lucid appraisal of Devlin's predicament. He spoke at length, describing the difficulties as he saw them and explaining in detail the options that were open to them. None of the options was exactly what might be described as soft. But then, Tanya reflected grimly as she watched the dark, aquiline profile with its harsh, unyielding lines, the man himself was clearly nothing if not hard. It was little wonder he was as spectacularly successful as he was. In addition to a quick, penetrating intelligence—which, in spite of herself, she could not but admire—he quite clearly also possessed in abundance the sort of single-minded ruthlessness that was so frequently the hallmark of those at the top. He offered her father an alternative to total shame—but he drove a hard bargain none the less.

His proposition was basically simple. He would buy Devlin's company from him. The business itself, of course, was worth nothing, but the name was one that still carried some weight in the art world and could prove valuable at some future date. The price he offered fell far short of the sum required to pay off Devlin's creditors, but to make up the difference he was prepared to provide a short-term, low-interest loan. On several conditions. First, Devlin would be required to take out a mortgage on his home and use the capital to set himself up gradually in business again—sufficient to begin repayment of the loan within a maximum period of six months after being declared medically fit. Further, until the loan was fully repaid, he must guarantee that all his investments would be made only with Cabrini's full approval, and that forty per cent of all profits from such investments would automatically go towards repayment of the loan.

Tanya listened silently. It was a neat and businesslike package. It let Devlin off the hook of bankruptcy—but it would bind him hand and foot for years to come. And as Cabrini sat back calmly in his chair, regarding Devlin from beneath dark brows as he waited for his answer, she felt a sudden wave of protectiveness towards the older man. He had already suffered so much.

Her father shifted in his chair and paused to take a deep breath before he spoke. 'I see,' he said at last. 'And I am most grateful to you, Signor Cabrini. I have no hesitation in accepting your fair and generous offer.'

'Generous!' The exclamation shot from her. 'I would hardly call Signor Cabrini's offer generous!'

The dark figure in the chair next to hers swivelled round to look at her. The eyes held hers with an expression of cool superiority. He's actually enjoying this, Tanya thought disgustedly as she struggled to meet steel with steel. It appeals to his sense of power to bring people to their knees.

'Is that so?' His eyes travelled insolently over her body as he spoke and, automatically, she winced away from him. 'And how would you describe it, *signorina*?' he enquired.

She glared at him. 'Hard, and a little soulless—like yourself.'

To her surprise, he smiled at that. 'And what were you hoping for, *signorina*? A handout? Did you expect me just to sign a cheque and hand it over on a silver plate?' The expression in his eyes was pure contempt.

'Of course not!' Tanya started to defend. 'My father would never have accepted such a thing!'

'That I know.' He swept her argument aside. 'But perhaps his daughter might not have been averse to it. You're used to having things easy, *signorina*, are you not? To snapping your fingers and being given exactly what you want? Correct me if I'm wrong.' He paused.

The coolly delivered insult caused Tanya to catch her breath. 'That's not true,' she bristled. It seemed as though the wretched man had done nothing but censure her from the moment she had walked in the door! And she turned to her father, hoping he would back her up. But he wasn't even listening. His head was bent over the sheet of rough calculations that Cabrini had sketched out. He seemed totally absorbed, oblivious. Angrily she swivelled round again to meet the dark, censorious eyes. 'I don't know where you get your information from, but I can assure you your sources are far from reliable. I am not in the habit of accepting handouts. I work for my living, just like you.'

He gave a low, derisive little laugh. 'I doubt if you even know what real work is. You strike me, *signorina*, as the type who takes a fairly leisurely and self-indulgent attitude to life. Somehow, I can't see you over-

stretching yourself.' A generous sprinkling of sarcasm
was in his voice as he pointed out, 'Any daughter who is
incapable of returning from a walk to be on time for an
appointment as important as this one is to your father
today, I would say is not in the habit of putting herself
out.'

Stung, Tanya blinked at him. 'I didn't mean to be
late,' she lied. He would only scorn her even more if she
tried to explain the reason why.

He smiled an irritating smile. 'I think,' he said, 'I've
made my point.' Then he surprised her by adding, 'I
understand you dabble in interior design? Perhaps you
were seeking inspiration in the great outdoors?'

That was unfair as well. Aside from all the other faults
he saw in her, he was branding her a mindless dilettante,
a gadfly professional beneath his dignity to take
seriously. And her professional reputation was something that Tanya held extremely dear. She straightened
abruptly in her chair and met his gaze with cool hostility.
'No—but I am a designer, if that's what you want to
know. Trained in London and Milan—though, unfor-
tunately, I was unable to complete my studies.'

She broke off, unwilling to reveal the reasons why.
Even now she found it painful to recall that time, that
dark day now almost two years ago when Devlin had
phoned her in Italy to tell her that her mother, his
beloved Natasha, was dead. Killed instantly when a lorry
had hit her car just a couple of miles from home. That
was when everything had started to go wrong, when her
father had started to fall apart.

But her voice was steady as she went on, 'Regrettably,
I haven't been able to develop my career to the extent I'd
have liked. You see, for the past two years I've been
working with my father, helping him to run the office
side of things.' She adjusted the wool dress over her

knees and sat back squarely in her seat. She had given a fairly good account of herself, she felt, though the very notion of having to justify herself to this arrogant man was nothing less than preposterous.

The dark gaze met hers, unimpressed. 'How unfortunate that your filial endeavours have resulted in such a resounding lack of success.' The cruel observation hung between them for a moment like an icy draught. Then he added very pointedly, 'A couple of months with me and you would really know what running a business was all about.'

It sounded remarkably like a threat. Tanya glared across at him with furiously narrowed eyes. 'I think I'd rather die!' she spat.

The dark eyes scanned her face, expressionless. Then his lips curved in a chillingly enigmatic smile. 'Tough words, *signorina*,' he observed. 'Let's hope you will not be required to eat them at some later date. They might prove somewhat indigestible.'

Precisely at that moment, Devlin chose to raise his head. 'There's one thing that bothers me,' he began, carefully laying the sheet of figures he had been studying to one side, apparently quite unaware that he was interrupting anything. His attention was focused solely on Cabrini now. 'The money that you have offered to lend me. You have no guarantee that I will ever pay it back.'

A faint smile played at the corners of the firm, well moulded lips and there was not a hint of malice now in the deep, smooth voice. 'I believe you to be a man of honour, Mr Sinclair. I trust you and I have every confidence that you will pay me back.'

But Devlin straightened in his chair and faced the younger man with dignity. 'I'm flattered by the compliment, but trust and confidence are not enough—

not in such matters where large sums of money are involved. I have few really valuable possessions left, Signor Cabrini, mostly paintings and other works of art. But, from what there is, I would ask you to take some piece, or pieces, of your choice as a kind of pledge on my part, a surety against my possible failure to repay your loan.' He paused and regarded Cabrini quizzically. 'Would that be acceptable to you?'

The dark head nodded. 'Perfectly acceptable—but quite unnecessary, I assure you.'

'I'm afraid I insist. Before we keep our appointment with my solicitors, I shall show you my little collection. It's mostly in the drawing-room.'

'No need. The piece I would choose is right here in this very room.' Fausto Cabrini paused and turned to Tanya with an unfathomable smile, and she winced away as he seemed to claim possession of her body with his eyes. Then his gaze slid away and she felt the muscles in her stomach slacken with irrational relief. For one ghastly, giddy moment she had feared he was about to make an outrageous demand! But her relief was painfully short-lived. Cabrini had leaned forward in his seat and was pointing to the little Russian icon that hung on the wall behind Devlin's head. 'That is the piece I would choose,' he said.

Tanya started forward, eyes flashing determinedly. 'You can't have that!' she burst out. 'That belonged to Grandpa Boris. It's a family heirloom. I'm sorry, Signor Cabrini,' she added, catching her breath. 'You'll have to choose something else.'

The dark eyes never moved from the little painting. 'It's a very fine example of eighteenth-century Russian iconography,' he offered in a mild voice, as though he hadn't heard a single word she had said. 'It will fit in very well with my collection at home.' And he turned to

Tanya with a triumphant smile.

'I'm afraid you haven't understood.' The tawny eyes flashed a warning at him. 'You can't have it.'

'And why might that be?' The dark gaze held hers levelly, a hint of mocking amusement in their inky depths.

'I told you, it's a family heirloom.' She paused and glanced across at the little work of art. Painted on wood in shades of gold and midnight-blue, it was probably Devlin's most prized possession and it had hung there on the wall behind his desk for the entire twenty-four years of her life. It had been a wedding present to her parents from her Russian-born grandfather Boris Karansky— one of the few family treasures the old man had managed to smuggle out of his homeland at the time of the Bolshevik revolution, and a sacred symbol for all these years of Devlin's union with his beloved Natasha. The very idea of allowing it to fall into the hands of someone like Fausto Cabrini was utterly unthinkable!

Her eyes swept back to the dark-suited figure seated next to her. 'Its value to my family is sentimental more than anything,' she offered, aware of the faintly pleading note that had crept into her tone of voice. 'Nothing could ever replace it. But you're more than welcome to take anything else.' Then, when he simply went on staring at her, granite-eyed, she anxiously turned towards her father for support. 'Tell him he can't have it, Father,' she implored.

Devlin looked uncomfortable and fumbled vaguely with the papers on his desk. 'I'd really rather you chose something else,' he said, carefully avoiding Tanya's gaze. 'As I said, there are several pieces in the drawing-room that you might like.'

But Fausto Cabrini shook his head decisively. 'I'm sorry, Mr Sinclair. The icon is what I choose.'

Devlin pursed his lips unhappily. 'An unfortunate choice, but if you insist . . .'

'I do.' Cabrini's coldly implacable expression never changed.

'In that case . . .' With a defeated sigh, Devlin rose stiffly from his chair and lifted the little icon from the wall. '. . . It is yours.'

Cabrini accepted the little masterpiece without a word, glanced at it only briefly before laying it to one side. And when he raised his eyes again their expression was as detached and businesslike as it had been before. 'Now I suggest we get back to the matter in hand,' he rapped. 'There are one or two points that need clarifying before we keep that appointment with your solicitors.'

Tanya eyed him with fierce dislike. How could a man like that ever begin to understand what the icon meant to her father? He was undoubtedly capable of assessing most things, and people, in terms of what they were worth in dollars and cents, but sentimental value, she guessed, would be a concept entirely alien to him. And, as she watched the dark brows knit in concentration as he bent over the sheet of figures on her father's desk again, she felt an icy shiver run through her bones. She had been right to call him soulless. That was exactly what he was.

Be that as it may, she had to admit the man was efficient. In less than a week all the legal loose ends of the agreement had been tied up and the bulk of Devlin's creditors paid off. Arrangements had also been made for Devlin to be flown to a private clinic near Lugano in Switzerland where Cabrini had insisted he would receive the best possible medical care. Tanya had smiled wryly to herself at that. He was prepared to go to any lengths, it seemed, to get her father on his feet again and paying back his wretched loan.

But at least the insufferable man was out of her hair. Two days after Renata's departure for New York, her brother had flown back to his base in northern Italy, with Tanya's blessing—and the fervent prayer that their paths would never cross again. Once had already been more than enough.

Now that her father's affairs were settled—at least as far as they could be—she planned to take a much-needed holiday. Perhaps to Austria, where some of her mother's relatives now lived. She had no desire to stay on in the Sussex house alone, and she had been promising to visit her Viennese relations for years. Now was as good a time as any and the break, she felt, would do her good.

Less than a week after her father had been flown to Switzerland, all her holiday arrangements had been made. Her clutch of cousins and aunts and uncles were all dying to see her, she had been assured, and she was welcome to stay in Austria all summer if she chose. For the first time in months Tanya felt her spirits rise. Her father was still far from out of the woods yet—but the worst of the crisis appeared to be past and she was determined to put her worries behind her for a while.

On the eve of her departure, as she settled down at home with a frozen pizza and a glass of wine to watch her favourite TV soap, she was feeling more optimistic than she had for quite some time. Tomorrow by lunch time she would be on her way. Free for a couple of months or so of all the recent sad events this house had seen. Free, too, to take some time to sort out in her mind exactly where she went from here. And perhaps, into the bargain, she might even manage to enjoy herself!

She laid down her plate impatiently as, suddenly, the doorbell rang. Who on earth could be visiting at this late hour? Reluctantly she hurried out into the hall, feeling her temper start to rise as the bell continued to clamour like a fire alarm. Whoever it was had simply stuck their finger on the bell and left it there!

Suspicious, she paused to peer through the spyhole before opening up—then in instant, angry recognition flung the door wide. 'What the hell do *you* want?' she demanded between clenched teeth.

Fausto Cabrini swept past her into the hall with a grim expression on his face. Then swung round to confront her with steely, dark eyes. 'You, *signorina*,' he informed her with an unpleasant smile. 'I'm afraid your presence is required in Italy.'

Instinctively Tanya found herself backing away. He had the look of a man whose temper was held on a very short leash. 'I don't know what you're talking about,' she spat at him. 'What the hell do you think you're doing, barging in here, demanding . . .?'

'I've already told you why I'm here,' he cut in on a menacing note. 'Just be grateful that I didn't smash the damned door down. I'm not in the mood for bandying words, *signorina*, so I'll get straight to the point.' He came towards her, the sides of his dark grey jacket flung back as he rested his hands belligerently on his hips. 'There's been an unexpected development, you see— one that demands a slight change in procedure on my part.' He paused less than a foot away from her, his face a smouldering mask of fury as he went on, 'You will recall that your father offered me a pledge to seal the contract that we made? Well, I intend *you* to be the token of that pledge.'

Tanya's eyes rounded in disbelief. 'But he gave you the icon,' she protested, wondering wildly if it was all a joke.

But Fausto Cabrini didn't laugh. The dark eyes narrowed in the harsh lines of his face and his voice held not the slightest trace of humour when he spoke. 'Yes, as you say, *signorina*, your father gave me the icon. And I, in good faith, accepted it.' He paused significantly before going on. 'But the icon, *signorina*, as you probably already know—is a fake.'

Tanya paled. 'A fake?'

'That's what I said, *signorina*. A beautiful, cleverly crafted and totally worthless fake.'

'But it can't be!' Tanya felt her blood grow cold.

'I'm afraid it is.' For a moment he just stood there, tight-lipped, and raked her face contemptuously with his stone-hard eyes. And a brief panic seized her as it seemed he might step forward and imprison her against the wall. But instead he stepped back and started to move towards the door. 'I have some business to attend to in London,' he rasped, 'but I shall be going back to Italy in two days' time.' He paused with one hand on the handle and spoke the final words of his dictum slowly so there was no danger of her misunderstanding him. 'I shall deny myself the pleasure of personally accompanying you—but make no mistake about it, *signorina*, when I get back to Italy I shall expect to find you there.'

CHAPTER TWO

THE sleek, black limousine slowed just a fraction as it turned off the main road and swept smoothly up to the tall, wrought-iron portals that guarded the entrance to the Cabrini estate. The chauffeur touched a button on the instrument panel in front of him and, in an almost imperious response, the huge gates swung silently open to let them pass.

Tanya felt a little knot of apprehension tighten in her breast. She leaned forward from the rich, deep comfort of the car's rear seat and addressed the back of the chauffeur's head. 'Are we here?' she enquired, managing to sound a lot more casual than she felt.

The peak-capped head nodded politely in response. '*Si, signorina, siamo arrivati.*' He touched the remote control button again and the big gates swung shut behind them with an almost chilling finality. Just like the gates of some prison, Tanya reflected drily to herself.

She sat back in her seat with a resigned sigh and smoothed the skirt of her cotton dress over her knees. Yes, from the look of things, they had most definitely arrived. And she tossed a stray gold curl from her shoulder and smiled a wry smile as she wondered what further little displays of ostentation lay in store for her.

The wide, gravel driveway was lined with shady poplars, but between the trees Tanya caught glimpses of bright, massed flowerbeds and broad expanses of sunlit lawn. It looked quite beautiful, she acknowledged grudgingly. But then, not even the unscrupulous hand of Fausto Cabrini could despoil the God-given beauty of nature, she reflected philosophically. His powers were mercifully confined to earthly matters.

At last the Villa Cabrini itself came into view and, in spite of herself, Tanya let out a gasp of pleasure at the sight of it. It was not at all what she had been expecting. Big, yes—but, to her amazement, not in the least grandiose or showy. In fact, there was an almost rustic feel to it with its red-tiled roof and shimmering, pale-stuccoed walls. As though it had stood there on the lakeside as long as the surrounding trees and hills themselves, and belonged there just as naturally.

The big car drew to a silent halt in a cobbled forecourt lined with earthenware pots full of geraniums. She waited as the chauffeur slid from his seat and came round to open the rear door for her. 'Thank you,' she murmured, stepping outside and stretching her cramped limbs gratefully. The warm June sun felt welcome on her arms after the air-conditioned coolness of the Mercedes.

A grey-haired woman in an immaculately starched apron had appeared on the steps of the open front door. Fausto Cabrini's housekeeper, Tanya guessed—and obviously innocently primed for the arrival of her unwilling guest. She came bustling up to Tanya now, a broad smile of welcome lighting her plump, cheerful face. 'Signorina Sinclair, at last you are here!' she effused in remarkably fluent English. 'You must be tired after your journey. Come inside and let me show you to your room. Beppe will bring your bags.'

The woman made a signal to the chauffeur, then led the way into a high-beamed hall whose floor was paved with rosy-coloured marble tiles and strewn with fabulously beautiful silk Persian rugs.

A wide, curved staircase led to the first floor where Tanya's room was situated. The plump-faced house-keeper pushed open a door on the east landing and bade her enter. 'This is the blue room,' she informed Tanya smilingly. 'I think you'll find it comfortable.'

The room was more than comfortable, it was positively luxurious. The bed was vast and covered with a blue silk coverlet of exactly the same shade as the swagged silk curtains hanging at either side of the tall balcony windows. The thick, soft carpet underfoot was also blue and the silk-lined walls were hung with delicate watercolours in pale gilt frames. As she paused to gaze round at the understated opulence of it all, Tanya felt suddenly acutely aware of the crumpled and travel-weary state of her dress. The sooner she got under a shower and changed into something fresh the better, she decided. This was no condition in which to stray into the lion's den.

As though reading her thoughts, the housekeeper pushed open the door that led to the en suite bathroom with its blue-tiled floor and walls and matching ceramic fittings. 'I think you'll find everything you need here,' she told Tanya, indicating the shelves of expensive-looking toiletries behind the bath. 'If not, just let me know.'

Tanya managed a vaguely appreciative smile. 'Thank you. It all looks very comfortable indeed,' she said.

The plump face beamed with open pride—almost as though she were the proprietor of this luxurious domain, it occurred to Tanya, instead of just another of Fausto Cabrini's countless paid servants. 'Now let me explain about the telephones.' She touched Tanya's arm and led her over to one of the bedside tables that flanked the enormous bed. 'The white phone is for external calls. The blue one is the internal one.' She smiled. 'You see, every room in the house is connected through our own private little telephone system. You just press four for the kitchen, for example, or nine for the *signor*'s room. You'll find a list of all the numbers in this drawer here. It is very convenient, don't you think?'

'Oh, very,' Tanya agreed, making a mental note that nine was a number she would never press, not even accidentally. And how very typical of the *signor*, she added scathingly to herself. Who else but Fausto Cabrini could possibly require two telephones in every room?

'*Ecco gli baggagli.*' The chauffeur was standing in the doorway with her bags.

'Put them over there, Beppe.' A plump finger indicated a space by the mirror-fronted wardrobe, then the grey-haired woman turned to Tanya, her eyebrows lifting in surprise. 'Surely this isn't all your luggage?' she enquired.

Tanya nodded. The two small cases were indeed all that she had brought with her. Despite what the other woman obviously believed, she fully intended that her stay be brief. 'It's all I'll need,' she acknowledged politely. And mentally reaffirmed her promise to herself that she'd be gone within the week.

'I'll leave you now.' The grey-haired woman smiled again. 'Would you like me to send up some coffee, a cold drink—something to eat, perhaps?'

'No, thank you.' Tanya shook her head.

'Very well, but if there's anything at all you want, don't hesitate to ring. My name's Emma, by the way. The *signor* has instructed me to take good care of you till he returns. We're expecting him home about seven tonight—and dinner will be served at eight.'

'Thank you, Emma, but I don't need anything right now. I think I'll just shower and unpack.'

'Come down whenever you're ready, my dear, and just make yourself at home. The *signor* insists that you treat this house as though it were your own.'

How generous of him, Tanya scoffed angrily to herself as the door closed and she was left alone. And how utterly hypocritical! How could she make herself at home when she was virtually a prisoner?

She crossed to the balcony windows and opened them wide. Breathing in deeply, she tried to calm the anger and resentment that were throbbing inside. The view, at least, was spectacular, she consoled herself. Smooth lawns bordered by shrubs and beds of flowering plants swept down to a wooded area near the water's edge. And, beyond that, stretched magnificent Lake Maggiore, sparkling like a jewel in the early summer sun. She could even glimpse in the distance the cloud-capped peaks of the Italian Alps. It was ironical to think that just a few kilometres on the other side, in a hospital bed in Switzerland, lay the man she loved more than any other in the world—and yet who was unwittingly responsible for her current, highly uncomfortable predicament.

She sighed and crossed to the blue-tiled bathroom, kicking off her shoes. Well, at least she had followed Cabrini's ridiculous orders to a tee—picked up her airline ticket at the airport just before the flight and arrived here at the villa several hours ahead of him. He should have no cause for complaint with her this time for a change. With any luck, the unfortunate mix-up about the icon would be sorted out without delay and that would be the end of the whole ghastly charade. She switched on the shower and quickly peeled off her clothes, then stepped with a grateful sigh under the warm, invigorating spray.

It was precisely at that moment that one of the phones in the bedroom began to ring. Cursing silently beneath her breath, Tanya grabbed the nearest fluffy blue towel and, wrapping it quickly round her dripping body, hurried through to answer it. A trail of water marked her path.

She picked up the white phone first—'Hello?'—but there was no one on the other end. She snatched up the blue one. 'Hello?' she said again, barely concealing the irritation in her voice.

'So you made it, *signorina*,' came Fausto Cabrini's smooth, sarcastic tones. 'You took so long to answer I thought perhaps you were having a nap.'

And no doubt took great pleasure in deliberately waking her. 'I was in the shower, actually,' Tanya responded, taking equal pleasure in disappointing him.

'And I interrupted you. I do apologise.' A note of amusement sounded in his voice. 'I hope you're not dripping soapsuds all over my carpet.'

Tanya glanced down at the soggy puddle at her feet. 'As a matter of fact, I am,' she enlightened him with blatant relish in her voice.

'In that case, I won't detain you any longer. Finish your shower and meet me in the library in half an hour.'

The phone went dead. Tanya glared at it in fury for a moment, then slammed the receiver down. So he had started his bullying tactics already! Muttering rebelliously to herself, she retraced her sopping footprints back to the bathroom.

Cabrini had a shock coming. There was no way she was going to stand for that!

Tanya almost didn't notice him at first. He was standing by the open library window with his back to her, but he wheeled round instantly at the sound of the closing door. 'Ah, there you are, *signorina*,' he greeted her without moving from the spot. 'I see you managed to find your way.'

She paused in the middle of the room, confronting him. 'If you mean to the library, I asked Emma the way. If you mean to the villa, your very efficient chauffeur took care of that.'

He smiled that amused, superior smile that she remembered from their first meeting. 'How very reassuring to know that my staff are taking such good care of you. But please don't stand there in the middle of the room—be seated.' And he indicated one of the deep-cushioned, soft leather armchairs that stood in a semi-circle round a low, brass coffee-table.

She automatically pulled back her shoulders and straightened her spine as she crossed to the armchair and sat down. He was even taller than she remembered. Broader, too. And as she was wearing flat-heeled sandals he towered over her. She made a mental promise to herself that next time she had the misfortune to be summoned to his presence she would make sure that she was wearing six-inch heels.

'Since I got back early and there's a couple of hours before dinner yet, I thought we might discuss your position here over a drink.'

'How very civilised. Not your usual style of doing things at all.' He was still standing over her. She did not look up. Instead, she glanced round quickly at the handsome, book-filled cabinets that lined the walls. The taste displayed in the furnishings elsewhere was equally evident in here. She added crisply, 'Our little discussion, however, should not take long. The whole thing's a dreadful mistake, you see.'

He crossed to a table behind her and she heard the clink of glasses. 'What will you have?' he enquired over his shoulder, taking no apparent notice of anything she had said.

Damn the man! She pursed her lips impatiently. 'A martini will do.'

He stood in front of her and handed her a tall glass with plenty of ice and a green olive stuck on the end of a cocktail stick. She took a mouthful. It was perfect, just as she liked it. But then, she acknowledged irritably to herself, that was exactly how she had expected it to be. Perfection was Fausto Cabrini's trademark, after all—at least when it came to the superficialities of life. She put her glass down on the table and lifted her eyes to him challengingly. 'Well? Why have you brought me here?'

He had seated himself in the armchair opposite, the ankle of one linen-clad leg hooked casually over the knee of the other, and he was watching her. Though apparently with no intention of responding to her demand. She stared back, registering how the pale colours of the open-necked shirt and lightweight trousers he wore made him seem younger than he had appeared in the dark suits he had worn in Sussex. She guessed that he was barely thirty-five.

'I must apologise for getting you out of the shower.' He took a mouthful of his drink and eyed her provocatively over the rim of his glass. 'That must have been most inconvenient for you.'

'Don't worry,' she retorted coolly. 'The only thing to suffer was your carpet.'

He raised an eyebrow at her and smiled. 'Carpets can easily be replaced—but we wouldn't want our young guest catching cold.' The dark eyes roamed insolently over her body, stripping her bare. 'I hope you took the time to grab a towel.'

She felt her colour deepen. The touch of his eyes was like a wanton caress. She glared at him across the coffee-table. 'I'm not your guest, Signor Cabrini, and I thought the purpose of this meeting was to discuss the futility of my presence here—not my health. As I've already pointed out to you, you've made a terrible mistake.'

He shook his head. 'I'm afraid it is not I, *signorina*, who have made a mistake. You are here for a very good reason—because your father cheated me.' Then he paused and fixed her with a cruel eye. 'And that, *signorina*, I promise you, was a very foolish mistake to make.'

'That's nonsense!' Suddenly Tanya was sitting bolt upright in her chair, eyes flashing at him angrily. 'My father never cheated anyone in his life! You're the one who's playing some sort of dirty game, inventing this ridiculous story about the icon being a fake!'

He continued to watch her in silence for a moment—but the black eyes had narrowed and the expression in them was cold and dangerous. He circled the rim of his glass with a sun-browned forefinger, an exercise, she felt instinctively, in self-control. 'Your loyalty to your father is most touching,' he said at last. 'But sadly misplaced, I fear. There is no doubt at all that the icon is a fake.' He reached into the pocket of his shirt and drew out a folded slip of paper, unfolded it carefully and handed it across the table to her. 'I think you have enough Italian to understand what's written here.'

She almost snatched the piece of paper from his hand and anxiously bent to study it. The letterhead bore the name of one of the most reputable auction houses in Milan—her father had dealt with them often in the past—and typed below was an expert appraisal of the icon, signed and dated and officially stamped. As Tanya read it, she felt the blood drain from her face.

'As you can see,' she heard Cabrini say, 'your father's little work of art is just a clever but worthless fake. Not eighteenth century at all, but probably made some time around the turn of the twentieth century. Though it took an expert to uncover the fraud.'

'But it can't be!' Tanya stared numbly at the piece of paper in her hand. That icon formed part of the essential folklore of her life. Since childhood she had listened to the story that old Grandpa Boris used to tell about how it had been sewn into his young wife's petticoats when the pair of them—along with the luckier members of their family—had fled from revolution-torn Russia back in 1917. It had been in the Karansky family for generations, he had always said. A valuable heirloom, as well as a sacred symbol of Devlin and Natasha'a love. Slowly she raised her eyes to meet Cabrini's again. 'I don't believe it,' she said.

He gave her a callous look. 'Believe what you wish. The truth remains.' He took the piece of paper from her and tossed it aside. 'And since I would undoubtedly consider your father to be an expert in this field, I can only conclude that he knew the icon was a fake—and that he cheated me deliberately.' He looked down at his glass and seemed to study it for a while. Then glanced up with a cutting smile. 'So you see, *signorina*, it is not I who have been playing dirty games. If I hadn't taken the icon to be valued—out of simple curiosity—I might never have discovered the little trick your father played on me.'

Tanya dropped her eyes uncomfortably. She somehow doubted very much that Cabrini had sought a valuation out of 'simple curiosity'. He was far too calculating for simple gestures of any kind. But, all the same, she realised that that was really not the point. 'There must be some explanation for all this,' she said. 'I'm sure my father would never have cheated you deliberately.' Then she added with a cautious smile, 'When I get back to England I'll arrange for some replacement paintings to be sent to you.'

Very slowly Fausto Cabrini shook his head. 'That, *signorina*, was not the solution I had in mind.' He stetched his long legs out in front of him. 'As I explained when I came to visit you in Sussex only the other night, I expect *you* to take the place of the icon. *You* will be the living token of your father's pledge.' A faint, humourless smile curled at his lips. 'Perhaps you didn't think that I was serious?'

Well, he couldn't be. Could he? She stared at him uneasily. 'That's ridiculous,' she said. 'I can't stay here. I've made arrangements to spend the summer with my relatives in Austria.'

He seemed to find that amusing. The corded muscles of his neck stood out against the deeply suntanned skin as he threw back his head in a rich, masculine laugh. 'Then you must un-make them, *signorina*,' he said simply. 'I shall require your presence here.'

'As a kind of hostage, you mean?' Her tone was clipped. 'How very Mediterranean.'

A faintly superior smile lingered around his lips. 'You have a sharp tongue, *signorina*,' he said, the dark eyes scanning her from head to foot. 'One of your less attractive attributes, I'd say. I shall take pleasure in teaching you some manners while you're here.'

The realisation was gradually dawning on Tanya that he was absolutely serious. He actually was enough of a megalomaniac to believe that he could force her to stay on with him. 'You must be mad!' She laid down her drink and squared her shoulders as she stared defiantly across at him. 'I have no more intention of staying on here than I have of going to the moon. And to prove it I'm going back to England on the first flight available—and from there I shall be going on to Vienna precisely as planned.'

'I'm afraid you won't, *signorina*.'

'Try to stop me!' She got to her feet.

'You mean like this?' He reached out easily and grabbed her by the wrist, the movement so swift and unexpected that she had no time to snatch her arm away. And he smiled with savage satisfaction as she struggled helplessly. 'You're going nowhere, *signorina*. Why don't you sit down?'

The lean, brown fingers were fastened round her slim wrist like a vice. In a passion of fury, she tried to pull free. 'How dare you, you bastard! Let me go!'

'Then sit down and listen to what I have to say.'

'Why should I?' She gave her arm a mutinous wrench—which merely forced him to tighten his grip.

'Let me go immediately! You're hurting me! There's nothing you could possibly have to say that I would want to listen to. You can't keep me here! Unless of course you intend to tie me up and keep me as your prisoner!'

'I have a feeling that will not be necessary.' Abruptly Fausto Cabrini rose to his feet and, with a sharp flick of his wrist, he twisted her arm behind her back so that she was virtually immobilised. The knuckles of his fist ground sharply into the small of her back as he jerked her towards him like a rag doll and held her there. 'Let me put it this way, *signorina*,' he gritted, the sudden closeness of their bodies lending an almost sensuous intensity to his words. 'I think I'm in a slightly stronger position than you when it comes to laying down the odds.'

He had her almost jammed up against him, so that she could feel the searing warmth of him, smell in her nostrils his clean, male smell. The dark eyes only inches from her own flamed with some untamed passion as he went on to warn, 'Your father and I have made a deal, a deal which I think you would agree is of considerably more importance to you and him that it is to me. If I should decide to withdraw from our deal—which I will unless you do exactly as I say—I think you might both live to regret the consequences bitterly.' He tightened his fingers sharply around her wrist as though to emphasise his point. 'Now, *signorina*, will you sit?'

Tanya grimaced and made one final, futile effort to pull away from him. 'You damned bully!' But she knew she was beaten and so did he.

'I asked you a question. Will you sit down and listen to what I have to say?'

She glared at him with every ounce of loathing that she felt. 'I don't really think I have much choice.'

'Good. I was pretty sure it wouldn't take you long to realise which side your bread was buttered on.'

He released her then quite suddenly, so that Tanya half stumbled back into her chair. For a moment she sat furiously rubbing the red mark on her wrist. Then she raised her eyes and spat across at him, 'So you've established that you can make me stay.' Of course she could never take the risk that he might leave her father in the lurch. 'But what I'd really like to know is *why* you want me here?'

'Certainly not for any pleasure I'm likely to derive from your company.'

So that much was mutual.

He sat down in his seat again and took another mouthful of his drink. 'Spoiled English brats, you see, are really not my cup of tea.'

She threw him a look of total contempt. 'And arrogant bullies of any nationality are very definitely not mine.'

'However,' he carried on smoothly, as though she had never opened her mouth, 'I'm prepared to put up with the sheer inconvenience of having you around in exchange for the sweeter and more subtle pleasures of revenge.' The dark eyes locked with hers as he elaborated on a malicious note, 'No one cheats me, *signorina*, and gets away with it. And, since your father is temporarily unavailable for the purpose of providing recompense, I am prepared to accept the services of his daughter in his place. Besides, I seem to recall the somewhat adamant manner in which you insisted on being included in the settlement of his affairs. I realise, of course, that at that time you were looking to a share in whatever handouts might come along—but I have no doubt that your filial devotion extends to the sharing of your father's liabilities as well.' He raised a taunting eyebrow at her. 'So now do you see why I feel I have no need to tie you up—and every confidence that you will stay here of your own free will?'

Tanya was almost choking with rage. 'Free will! Is

that what you call it? It sounds a lot more like blackmail to me.'

He shook his head dismissively. 'You can call it what you like, it really doesn't matter to me. What matters is that you stay.'

Tanya reached out a shaky hand for her drink and took a long, slow, steadying sip. 'How long do you intend to keep me here? And how am I supposed to provide this *recompense* that you require?' She emphasised the word distastefully and stared across at him with all the scorn that she could muster in her tawny eyes.

He merely smiled. 'You shall repay me in whatever manner I require.' And paused to let the threat implicit in his words sink in. 'For a start, you can help me in the office here. By a curious coincidence I lost my regular secretary rather suddenly some weeks ago. I take it you know how to type and answer the phone? That much you must have mastered while you were in your father's employ. And I believe you have enough Italian to get by.'

Tanya said nothing. She felt like a fly caught in a spider's web.

He continued with a triumphant smile, 'The arrangement has much to commend it, don't you think? We have already established that you have a lot to learn about running a business successfully. I shall take considerable pleasure in instructing you.' Then he added, with a glint of venom in the hard, dark eyes, 'You may be assured that your stay here will be no holiday. By the end of it, you will undoubtedly have come to appreciate the true meaning of hard work.'

He was so damned smug! So infuriatingly confident of his own unshakable superiority! And there seemed to be no way that Tanya could get back at him. She threw him a scathing look. 'No doubt the slave-driver's whip will sit extremely comfortably in your hand. I would say it's a role that you're eminently suited to.'

'No doubt.' A flicker of amusement crossed the dark-tanned face. 'Of course, whether or not I need to use the whip is entirely up to you. There's no reason why our relationship as employer and employee should not be perfectly amicable.'

'Employee?' she scoffed. 'A quaint expression to use for someone who's been press-ganged into working for you.'

'As I said, it's up to you. If you insist on refusing to co-operate, we shall soon see who is going to suffer more.' He spoke the words harshly and underlined them with a caustic smile. 'I promise you one thing, it will not be me.'

She said nothing, just sat there silently, hating him.

He continued in that maddeningly gloating tone of voice, 'You'll be pleased to learn that you'll be working here, from the villa. This is where I'm based during the summer months.'

So she was to be confined like a prisoner on the estate. Things were going from bad to worse. She raised a sceptical eyebrow at him. 'Don't tell me you manage to control the entire Cabrini empire from a little room on the banks of Lake Maggiore?' Not even he, surely, would be capable of that.

'More or less. It's amazing what modern technology will allow. As I shall show you tomorrow, I have a very well equipped office downstairs.'

Tanya fixed him with a baleful stare. Surely he didn't actually expect her to be interested!

But he appeared to be indifferent whether she was or not. 'As you'll discover,' he went on, draining his glass, 'I tend to leave the day-to-day running of our various industrial interests to my cousins in Milan—and concentrate largely on my private investment consultancy. That's what you'll be involved with principally.'

'Investment consultancy!' Tanya squared her shoulders aggressively. 'And why do you need a private investment consultancy? Weren't all the Cabrini millions enough for you?'

He gave her a long, slightly unnerving look before laying down his empty glass and leaning across the table, equally aggressively, to answer her. 'Why do I need it? For the sorts of reasons that you, *signorina*, are never likely to understand. To prove to myself that I could stand by my own efforts and abilities. That I didn't need the Cabrini millions. That I was perfectly capable of making millions of my own.'

'How worthy.'

'As I said, it isn't something I'd expect someone like you to comprehend.' Then, 'How much do you know about that line of business anyway?'

'Not a lot. You fiddle around with dollars and yen, play the stock markets and make vast profits from your already wealthy clients. And yourself, of course.' She paused, pleased with the note of naked censure in her voice. 'Am I close?'

'Close enough—for the moment.' He reached across the table suddenly and took her glass. 'Allow me to freshen your drink for you.'

That was rich! The great Fausto Cabrini actually suggesting that he might require her permission for something!

'Your drink.' Suddenly he was standing over her, the sun-bronzed fist clutching the proffered glass less than a handspan from her face. And she had to steel herself from flinching at the strange sensation his proximity had stirred in her. Part resentment, part something else.

'Thank you.' She reached for the glass and, just for a heartbeat, his fingers lightly brushed against her own. His touch was like an electric current jolting through her. Even more shocking, somehow, than that earlier, more abrasive encounter had been. And she gasped and jerked her hand away—and splashed martini all over her lap. Damn! She cursed silently. Now she was making a fool of herself.

He reached into the pocket of his pale linen trousers and produced a large white handkerchief. 'Shall I mop it up for you?'

'I'd rather you didn't.' Her tone was cool, though she hated the way her face had flamed.

'As you wish.' He dropped the handkerchief into her hand and turned away. But she could tell without even glancing up at him that he was throughly enjoying her embarrassment. Furiously she dabbed at the wet mark.

'I shouldn't worry too much about that.' He lowered his tall frame into his seat again. 'Emma's an expert at dealing with these little catastrophes.' Then he raised his glass and smiled provocatively across at her. 'Here's to our little agreement,' he said. 'May it prove beneficial to us both.'

Tanya abandoned her efforts with the handkerchief and drank without acknowledging his toast. This so-called agreement had been reached because she had a shotgun at her head. She could think of nothing more pernicious than being stuck here in the wilds of northern Italy with this bloody-minded man.

But it was more than just simple resentment that she felt. There was something about this man that disturbed her, something that caused her to react to him in a manner she could not understand. For it wasn't simply that she detested him. There was more to it than that— something deeper, more elemental—and, though she couldn't quite put her finger on it, it alarmed her somehow. Again she had that instinctive feeling that Fausto Cabrini was dangerous.

Almost defensively she turned to the attack and forced herself to meet the dark, discomfiting gaze. 'You haven't answered my question yet. How long do you intend to keep me here?'

'That depends, *signorina*, on a number of things. On how long it takes you to learn the several lessons I intend to teach you while you're here. On your father's progress. Once he's recovered and starting to pay off his debt to me I'll have no more cause to hold you here as my indemnity. And on how long it takes me to find a suitable replacement for my lately departed secretary.' He paused, enjoying her discomfort, before concluding with a pitiless smile, 'I would say that by the end of the summer I should be able to let you go.'

Tanya's heart sank. 'The end of the summer? That's months away.'

'Three months, more or less. But don't worry, it'll pass quickly enough. You're going to be so busy that, I promise you, the time will fly.' He drank back half his drink, then went on, studying the expression on her face with interest as he spoke, 'Your duties will not be confined to daytime, of course. There will be occasions when I shall require you to accompany me in the evening to some dinner or other function. I take it you have no objection?' he added lightly, almost as an afterthought.

Tanya felt her fingers tighten angrily around her glass. Why, the inconceivable cheek of the man! 'I'm afraid I do have an objection,' she informed him tight-lipped. 'I'm not some kind of escort agency, you know. I shall work for you in your office if you insist, but don't get any ideas about extending our relationship into the social field.'

'*Signorina*, I think it is you who are getting ideas, not me.' Fausto Cabrini looked across at her impatiently and ran a strong, brown finger down the straight line of his nose. 'The little outings I alluded to are all part of the job. In England you may be used to working strictly nine

to five—that is, when you work at all—but I'm afraid
that I don't operate like that. Nor do I confine my
professional activities to the office. You will discover
that working dinners and lunches are a regular part of
my routine—as they will be of yours as long as you're
working for me. So you'd better just get used to it.
However, have no fear, *signorina*, I have no plans to
extend our relationship as you suggest.'

And the fine mouth twisted derisively as he delivered
his final point. 'Believe me, if what I was after was some
girl to dangle gracefully on the end of my arm, I
wouldn't need to go to the lengths of employing the
services of an escort agency. I have never found it
necessary to pay for any service that a woman can
provide.'

Tanya glared across at him with a burning dislike.
Any woman who voluntarily had anything to do with a
man like him must be out of her mind ! And more than
just mad, a raving masochist as well! 'Well, whether it's
part of my job or not, I'm afraid I won't be able to
oblige.'

'And why might that be? Let's see——' And he raised
one darkly quizzical eyebrow as he went on. 'You have a
possessive boyfriend back home who would object—is
that it?'

'Nothing like that,' she answered truthfully. There
was no boyfriend back home with any particular claims
on her affections or fidelity. Never had been, really,
though it occurred to her that whether there were or not
was none of Fausto Cabrini's affair. 'The reason is much
more straightforward than that. I don't have anything to
wear. All I brought with me were a few casual clothes.
Nothing remotely suitable for the elegant little *soirées*
I'm sure you have in mind.' There was a note of triumph
in her voice. It had turned out to be a blessing indeed

that she had brought such a modest supply of clothes with her.

He simply shrugged. 'No problem. There are a couple of cupboards full of Renata's clothes upstairs. I'm sure you'll find plenty to fit you there. And if you don't——' he threw her a calculatedly irritating smile '—we simply go out and buy you something suitable.'

At that point, Tanya could gladly have thrown her glass at him. Did the wretched man have an answer for everything? She stared at him sullenly—then a sudden question crossed her mind. A question some instinct told her he might not be able to dispose of quite so easily. 'Why did your other secretary leave? You said she left quite suddenly.'

'Yes, she did leave somewhat abruptly. I dare say she had her reasons.'

'Didn't she tell you what those reasons were?'

'She may have done.' Already there were angry warning signals flashing from his eyes.

'So tell me what they were.'

He leaned forward in his seat and studied her for a long moment, and his tone was flint-hard when he spoke. 'My dear *signorina*, I think we should get one thing perfectly clear. I have a particular aversion to people who pry—especially women—so I suggest you drop this line of questioning.'

But perversely Tanya was enjoying the angry reaction she had provoked. For once it almost felt as though she had got him on the hop. 'Surely that was a perfectly harmless thing to ask,' she protested in mock-innocence.

The dark eyes narrowed and the lines around his mouth were hard. 'So you insist?'

She faced him out, determined not to let him frighten her. 'I can't understand why such an innocuous little question should bother you so much. What's the matter, have you got something to hide?'

'Apparently you weren't listening. I've told you once already that I don't wish to discuss the subject—and I don't like having to repeat myself!' Impatience rose in his voice. .

'Oh, is that so! Well, maybe you're used to people snapping to attention and always doing exactly as you say, but don't expect that sort of thing from me. I don't give a damn what you're used to or how you think I should behave. I can just imagine why your secretary left. What did you do to her, you bully?'

The knuckles clamped round his tumbler had gone very white and his tone was as jagged as broken glass as he ground out, 'Don't go too far, *signorina*. I'm warning you.'

She forced a brittle-sounding laugh. 'You mean you're threatening me! And what exactly do you intend to do? Give me another little demonstration of your physical superiority?'

He seemed to hover on the edge of his seat for a moment as though tempted to do exactly that. But instead he simply flayed her with a whiplash look. 'I'm sorry, *signorina*. Not tonight.' Then he swallowed back his drink in a single gulp and slammed the heavy glass down on the tabletop. 'I have a couple of things to attend to.' He glanced down quickly at the sliver of gold watch at his wrist and rose abruptly to his feet. 'I think I'll have dinner in my room tonight. You can make your own arrangements with Emma.' He paused and faced her with a ferocious stare. 'Kindly call your relatives in Austria—and anyone else who needs to know—and tell them you'll be staying here indefinitely. Tomorrow morning we start work at eight. I shall expect you in the office punctually.' Then, in a few, swift strides, he left the room.

For a full five minutes after he had gone Tanya remained in her seat, rigid with fury. To her intense annoyance she discovered that she was still clutching in one hand the handkerchief that he had given her. With all her strength she flung it angrily across the room. Why, Fausto Cabrini must be the most arrogant, objectionable male chauvinist it had ever been her misfortune to encounter in her entire life!

She stood up shakily and straightened her still-damp skirt. Well, two could play at that little game! He might have the upper hand, he might be in a position to force her to stay and work for him, but there was no way she would just sit back and allow him to push her around. For it wasn't just her Slavic good looks that Tanya had inherited from her mother, there was also more than a trace of the fiery Russian temperament flowing through her veins. The Sinclair in her might be gentle, generous and mild—but a Karansky could stand up to a Cabrini any day of the week.

The great Fausto might not be aware of it yet, but he had a battle on his hands!

CHAPTER THREE

IT was like walking into some highly exclusive Bond Street boutique. Silks and chiffons hung in clouds of glorious colour from the wardrobe doors; deep velvets and sequin-encrusted satins lay draped, like all the riches of Croesus, over the bed.

Emma grinned at her as she stood in the doorway open-mouthed. 'I came up ahead of you, *signorina*,' she explained, 'to look out a couple of things I thought might suit.'

A couple of things! Tanya suppressed a smile. She had always thought she had a pretty extensive wardrobe at home, but it was nothing compared to this. It was on Fausto Cabrini's instructions, naturally, that she had come.

An amused smile had flitted across his face as he'd told her, deliberately provocative, 'We have a dinner engagement with a couple of clients and their wives tonight. Have a look through Renata's wardrobe for something to wear.'

She had forced a totally impassive smile on to her face. 'I'll do that,' she had promised, secretly hating him with fresh vigour.

But none of that was Emma's fault. Tanya smiled gratefully at the grey-haired woman now. 'That's very good of you, but I don't think I'll be needing anything very special for tonight. As far as I understand, Signor Cabrini is only taking a couple of clients and their wives to dinner.'

'Ah!' The housekeeper shook her head and waggled a plump forefinger in mild admonishment. 'But he will not be taking them to some pizza parlour, *signorina*. He

46

will be taking them to one of Milan's most elegant restaurants—and for such an occasion it is a woman's duty to herself to make sure she is looking her very best.' She held up an aquamarine silk creation with softly draped bodice and slim, slightly tapered skirt. 'With your beautiful gold hair I think this will look spectacular.'

Once she had slipped it on and examined her reflection in the ceiling-to-floor mirror, Tanya more or less had to agree. It was the sort of dress that did marvels for a girl's morale.

'*Squisito!*' Emma pronounced, just in case she should have any doubts. 'I tell you, that dress was made for you. But now try this one.' She slipped a fine silk jersey gown in deep fuchsia from its hanger and handed it to Tanya. 'This one also will look very elegant on you.'

It did. And so did just about everything else that Tanya tried on. 'I think Renata has the most gorgeous collection of clothes I've ever seen,' she confessed to Emma over an hour and more than a dozen outfits later. 'I love every single one of them.'

Emma beamed as though the compliment had been directed at her. 'Indeed,' she agreed, slipping yet another astounding creation from its hanger and passing it to Tanya. 'Even as a little girl she always had the prettiest clothes.'

Tanya looked at the other woman in some surprise. 'You've known her *that* long?' she enquired curiously.

'Oh, yes. And her brother, the Signor Fausto, too. I went to work for their parents more than thirty years ago. That was in New York, of course.' She paused. 'Naturally you knew that the *signor* and the Signorina Renata were born in the United States?'

Tanya nodded. Renata had told her that. 'And when did you come back to Italy?' she asked.

Emma sighed. 'We all came back about ten years ago.

That was after the *signor's* mother died. A very sad time. My own husband was taken at about the same time and, mercifully, when the Signor Fausto and the Signorina Renata left New York to come over here and join their father in Milan, the *signor* persuaded his father to allow me and my young son to come back as well. I'd spent more than twenty years in the United States, but when my husband died I just wanted to come home again.' She paused as a wistful little smile lit up her face. 'I have a lot to be grateful to the *signor* for. As you know, the Signorina Renata returned to New York some years ago to make her home there—and I wasn't really needed in Milan. But when his father died and the *signor* took over this place he asked me to come and be his housekeeper. And he made my son Beppe assistant manager of the estate.'

'Beppe?' Suddenly Tanya remembered why the name had a familiar ring. 'Do you mean the young man who drove me from the airport? The chauffeur?'

Emma nodded with maternal pride. 'Yes, he chauffeurs for the *signor* as well, sometimes. Doesn't he look handsome in his uniform?'

Tanya vividly recalled the slim, dark youth who had stood out so spectacularly in the arrivals lounge. She nodded. 'Yes, he does.'

Again Emma smiled that wistful little smile. 'Sometimes I wonder what would have become of Beppe if it hadn't been for the *signor*. Soon after we returned to Italy it was discovered he was suffering from a very serious heart condition. He needed major surgery and a long stay in hospital—and the *signor*, bless him, paid for everything.' She pulled a handkerchief from her apron pocket and blew very loudly into it. 'Oh yes, I have a great deal to be thankful to the *signor* for.'

All this unrestrained adulation for Fausto Cabrini was beginning to make Tanya feel ever so slightly nauseous.

So what if he had ever-so-compassionately persuaded his father to bring Emma and Beppe back to Italy? It had probably suited his own purposes very nicely to do so. And so what if he had ever-so-generously paid all Beppe's medical bills? A few thousand pounds to a man of Fausto Cabrini's wealth meant absolutely nothing. Besides, he had probably been repaid a dozen times through the faithful, unstinting service that both Beppe and Emma had undoubtedly given him over the years. Yet here was Emma lavishing praise on the man as though he were some kind of latter-day philanthropist!

It made Tanya's blood boil. And it reminded her somewhat bitterly of her own father's misplaced gratitude. 'Signor Cabrini's generous offer', he had said—when in fact there had been nothing generous about the deal Cabrini had offered at all. Yet making others feel beholden to him was quite clearly Fausto Cabrini's stock in trade. No doubt it appealed to his overweening sense of power and superiority. He enjoyed the role of big man dispensing favours, the *grande signor* impressing the peasants with his magnificent largesse.

Tanya sniffed derisively to herself as she stepped out of the final dress that Emma had picked out for her. Well, she for one was never likely to be taken in. She had seen the cold, hard, calculating other side of him. She knew him for the tyrant that he really was.

Emma was watching her expectantly. 'Have you decided, *signorina*?' she enquired as Tanya handed the last dress back to her.

Tanya hesitated. 'They're all so beautiful.' Then added with sudden decision, 'But I think the first one, the aquamarine silk.'

'A perfect choice,' Emma agreed. 'With your colouring it looks magnificent.' She started gathering up the piles of dresses and hanging them back in the wardrobes again. 'I'll press it for you and leave it in your room. And the fuchsia and the white as well. These will come in handy for future occasions.'

Tanya mentally wrinkled her nose at the thought. In the sheer delight of trying all the dresses on she had quite forgotten the unfortunate purpose behind the exercise. A working night out with Cabrini—and only the first of many, she feared. With a sudden stab of resentment she decided to take her opportunity to embark on a subtle line of investigation about the man. 'It's really very nice of Signor Cabrini to take me along on this dinner tonight,' she confided to Emma, hoping the false words at least sounded sincere. Then added ultra-casually, 'Used he to take his previous secretary on these little outings too?'

'Oh yes. From time to time. I think she enjoyed them. I'm sure you will too, *signorina*.'

'I'm sure I shall,' Tanya lied—then quickly asked the question she had been leading up to all the time. 'Why did she leave?' The question had been bothering her since Cabrini had revealed himself so reluctant to be drawn on the subject yesterday—and it struck her as more than likely that Emma would know the reason why.

Just for a moment the smile seemed to fade from the housekeeper's plump, good-humoured face and Tanya thought she detected a trace of embarrassment in the hurried reply. 'She went back south to her family. She came from a village in Calabria, you see.'

'But why would she want to go back there if she had a good job here?' Tanya insisted, certain that Emma was hiding the truth. It seemed more than highly probable that the girl had left because of Cabrini. After all, it wasn't hard to imagine any employee reaching the point where she simply couldn't stomach his monstrous male arrogance any more. She had serious doubts about her own ability to put up with it. Or, possibly, he had fired the girl without notice on some vain, vindictive whim.

He was exactly the sort of bully who would do such a thing. And for some reason Tanya was curious to get to the bottom of the mystery.

The grey-haired woman shrugged as she carefully draped the three chosen dresses over her arm. 'She left, *signorina*. That is all I know.' And something in her tone warned Tanya it would be pointless to ply her with more questions. She clearly intended giving nothing away.

Abruptly, Tanya changed the subject. She had already been accused once of prying where this matter was concerned and she had no desire to have that particular accusation levelled at her again. She would find out the truth in time, no doubt. She threw Emma a conciliatory smile. 'Thanks for your help with the dresses. I really appreciate your taking the time.'

'My pleasure.' Emma returned her smile, evidently relieved that the subject of Tanya's predecessor had been dropped. 'And now I must go and get lunch ready.'

A table on the terrace had been laid for two under a huge red-and-green-striped sun umbrella. As Tanya stepped through the french doors of the dining-room on to the sunlit ceramic tiles, she noticed that Fausto Cabrini was already waiting for her. And the spindly high heels of the red strappy sandals she was wearing beat a sharp tattoo as she hurried over to join him. He at least had the grace to raise his eyes, if nothing else, as she sat down.

'I asked Emma to prepare something fairly light,' he told her, indicating with a brief wave of his hand the platters of *prosciutto, bresaola* and other cold meats arranged with a huge bowl of salad on the sparkling white tablecloth. Then he added, evidently not greatly concerned whether the arrangement suited her or not, 'We'll probably be having a pretty heavy dinner tonight.'

He had shed the jacket of the cream linen suit he had

been wearing in the office earlier, and the pale blue shirt, that somehow emphasised the darkness of his tan, was open at the neck and casually rolled back at the cuffs. As Tanya glanced across at him, she caught an unexpected glimpse of brown, hair-roughened chest. 'This will be fine,' she assured him and sat down quickly, averting her eyes.

He leaned forward and poured red wine from a carafe into her glass. 'Did you have any success with Renata's things?'

'Yes, thanks,' she answered, deliberately brief, and helped herself to a couple of slices of cold meat.

'Good.' She had expected that he would ask her to elaborate, but instead he dropped the subject and entreated her, 'I suggest you eat up. I have a very busy afternoon ahead and there's something I'd like to show you after lunch.'

'I'll be as quick as I can.' She threw him a sarcastic look and jammed a large piece of Parma ham on to the end of her fork. He had a nerve, virtually commanding her to have lunch with him, then, the minute she sat down to eat, instructing her to get the food down as fast as possible and not waste his precious time! She glared across the table at him and lifted the enormous forkful to her mouth.

'I'm glad to see the morning's work has given you an appetite. Still, there's no need to give yourself indigestion, I'm sure.' He was sitting back in his seat so that the expression on his face was lost in the shadow of the sun umbrella, but Tanya could hear the mocking amusement in his voice. The black eyes would be watching her through narrowed, disdainful lids, the firm lips curved in an even more disdainful smile. Defiantly she stuffed the fork and its exaggerated load into her mouth and proceeded to chew slowly and methodically, privately praying that she wouldn't choke. Let him laugh at her if he liked. She really didn't give a damn.

'Did you have time to look through those files I gave you?'

She finished chewing and swallowed carefully before answering. 'Of course.'

'Good. We can discuss the contents later.'

Tanya stabbed a slice of herbed tomato with her fork. So it wasn't enough that she had to suffer the imposition of working for him—she was to be subjected to regular cross-examinations as well! Though this morning, admittedly, he had left her pretty much to herself.

She had arrived at Cabrini's office on the lower ground floor at precisely seven minutes to eight—step one in her strategy to put paid to his eternal carping about her being some kind of spoiled and lazy brat. Not that he had bothered to comment on her commendably zealous punctuality. Instead, after a perfunctory greeting, he had told her, 'Let's get started. I'll show you round.'

Fausto Cabrini had most definitely been right about one thing, she had quickly discovered. His office in the converted basement of the villa was superbly equipped, even to the extent of boasting a sophisticated computer link-up with his offices in Milan. At the touch of a button he could summon up-to-the-minute details of Cabrini Industries' latest deal or see how the dollar was faring on the Hong Kong currency exchange. It was all rather impressive and a far cry from the 'little room on the banks of Lake Maggiore' that Tanya had so scathingly described.

Her own adjoining office, she'd been relieved to see, was much more modestly kitted out. Just an ordinary typewriter, a row of standard filing cabinets and a couple of phones. With any luck she would not be required to cope with any of the fancy electronic gadgetry next door.

It was almost as though he could see inside her head

now as he reached for a bread roll and broke it in two. 'Tomorrow I'll start teaching you how to use the computer,' he said. Then added, misinterpreting the look of irritation on her face, 'That, of course, will require a bit of unaccustomed effort on your part—but I'm afraid you won't really be a great deal of use to me otherwise.'

Tanya eyed him with hostility. Being 'of use' to Fausto Cabrini was really the very least of her desires. And the prospect of being subjected to his tutelage held absolutely no appeal at all. 'Couldn't you just give me a manual or something to study? I'm sure you're much too busy to waste time teaching me.'

'Oh, it will not be time wasted, *signorina*, I promise you.' Reading her thoughts with total accuracy this time, he went on, 'It need not even be particularly unpleasant if you're prepared to approach it in the right frame of mind.'

'The right frame of mind being one of total subservience to you, no doubt.'

'Not to me, *signorina*. To the task in hand. You may even somewhat belatedly discover that effort and achievement have their own rewards.'

Tanya watched as he dealt deftly with a large slice of *mortadella* and suddenly longed to wipe the look of smug superiority from his face. 'Are effort and achievement all you ever think about?' she asked him nastily. 'It seems to me you lead a very one-dimensional life.'

'Is that so?' One dark eyebrow arched in amused curiosity at her remark. 'And on which particular dimensions would you suggest my life is lacking, *signorina*?'

Tanya hesitated. Already she could sense that she was stepping into deeper water than she had meant, but she forced herself to plunge foolhardily on. 'Your work seems to take up your entire life. You give the impression that you really don't have a great deal of time for anything else.'

'Like what, for example? I swim and jog and play other sports. I listen to music regularly. I travel a lot.' He was taking obvious delight in cleverly leading her into an area where she did not want to go. 'Tell me, where is this great gap in my life that you perceive?'

She made a stab at what she hoped looked like a casual shrug. 'People, relationships—they don't seem to figure very much.'

'Relationships?' Fausto Cabrini repeated the word slowly, as though he had never actually come across it before. 'And what sorts of relationships exactly did you have in mind?'

Tanya squirmed inwardly, detesting the way he had manoeuvred her into a corner like this. She stared at him flatly. 'Normal relationships.'

'Normal relationships?' He frowned back at her.

'That's what I said.' The tawny eyes snapped impatiently at him. Did he intend to repeat every wretched thing she said?

'I see.' He feigned dawning enlightenment and leaned towards her with an almost rakish smile. 'So it's the sexual dimension that you're curious about.'

'I didn't say that.'

'You didn't need to.'

God, how she hated him!

'Still, let me set your mind at rest,' he told her with satisfaction, overriding the feeble protest that was forming on her lips. 'That particular dimension of my life is well taken care of.' A wicked gleam shone in his eyes. 'Of course, if you insist I'd be perfectly happy to elaborate.'

'I'd really rather you didn't, thank you all the same. I have no wish to know the sordid details of your life.'

'Good.' He helped himself to another couple of slices

of cold meat. 'I doubt that either of us can really spare the time.'

For the rest of the meal Tanya concentrated on the food in front of her, though their little skirmish had somewhat blunted her appetite. Of course, she might have known that he would end up getting the better of her. For some intolerable reason he always did. He for ever seemed to be at least two jumps ahead of her. It was his devious nature, she decided, watching with cold distaste from the corner of her eye as he devoured with tranquil relish the generous pile of food heaped on his plate. He was a born manipulator, a man who would never let scruples hold him back.

For the moment, however, he seemed as happy as she to eschew further confrontation—though she had no illusions that this peaceful, almost conciliatory mood would last.

It was later, as Emma appeared to clear away the coffee things, that he suddenly pushed back his chair without warning and got to his feet. 'Shall we go?' It was less of a suggestion, more of a command.

Tanya blinked at him. 'Go where?'

'I told you there was something I wanted to show you.'

'Of course.' It had totally slipped her mind.

He started to move away impatiently, heading for the steps that led down from the terrace into the garden.

She hurried after him. 'Where are you taking me?'

He paused at the foot of the steps and turned to look up at her. 'You'll see.' Then he flicked a critical glance at the precariously heeled sandals she was wearing. 'Don't you have anything a bit more sensible to put on your feet? The ground's pretty rough where we're headed.'

Tanya tossed her head dismissively. This morning she had deliberately picked out the highest-heeled pair of sandals that she'd brought with her. And it had been a complete and utter waste of time. Even with these veritable stilts, he still managed to tower over her! 'Thank you, but I can manage perfectly well in these,' she retorted, both irked and curious at the same time. Where on earth was he taking her?

He shrugged. 'Suit yourself.' Then turned away. 'Just follow me—and watch where you put your feet. I don't want to end up having to carry you because you go and turn your ankle.'

Perish the thought! She hurried down the stone steps behind him, secretly vowing that even if she broke both legs she would crawl back on all fours before she would allow Fausto Cabrini the satisfaction of gallantly coming to her aid. She would almost sooner die than that.

All the same, she soon found herself wishing she were wearing slightly more comfortable heels as she followed his tall frame across the lawn and past the flowerbeds to the wooded area where the grounds directly overlooked the lake. He was making no concessions at all—neither for her shorter legs, nor for her ridiculously unsuitable footwear—and Tanya was finding considerable difficulty in keeping up with him. Had he been anyone else, she would have called out, asked him to slow down a bit—but, instead, she simply gritted her teeth in silence and staggered on as best she could.

They had come to the edge of the wooded area and abruptly he came to a halt and whirled round to face her. She jumped back, startled, and felt herself flush, foolishly wondering if he had had secret access to her thoughts.

Apparently he hadn't, for there was only cool detachment in the dark eyes that met hers. 'The ground's a bit rough from now on,' he informed her. 'Perhaps you might find it easier if you went barefoot.'

She stared past him and straightened her shoulders

mutinously. 'That won't be necessary. I told you I can manage.'

He turned away again without a word and led the way along a narrow, winding path between the trees. Maybe he had increased his pace, or maybe Tanya was simply finding it more and more of a struggle to keep up with him, but on more than one occasion he completely disappeared from view and she had no choice but to stumble blindly on, keeping her eyes peeled for the occasional, reassuring patch of blue that at least told her she was heading in the right direction.

The straps of her sandals had almost rubbed her feet raw in places, but she absolutely refused to take them off. She would sooner cripple herself, she decided with a perverse kind of determination, than admit to Fausto Cabrini that he had been right.

She was close to the point of submitting, though, and kicking off the wretched things when the path led out unexpectedly into a brightly sunny clearing amid the trees. At the back of the clearing stood a small, three-storey building—and in the open doorway, arms folded, silently watching her, a tall, dark figure in a pale blue shirt. 'So you made it,' he remarked, barbed amusement in his voice. 'I was just about to send out a search party.'

'No need, I assure you. I'm perfectly able to look after myself.'

He threw her a darkly disbelieving look. 'I doubt, *signorina*, that that has ever been truly put to the test. But now that you're here, let me show you what I brought you for.' He stepped out of the doorway and came towards her, and automatically she moved away. If he noticed, he made no sign of it, but turned to look up at the little building with its typically Italian ochre-painted walls, green-shuttered windows and sloping, red-tiled roof.

'This used to be the wash-house for the estate in the

days when the old *baroni* used to rule the roost around these parts. They got the water from the lake, then heated it in the huge wood-fired boilers on the ground floor. On the first floor was where everything was actually washed, and then——' he pointed upwards '—it was hung out on the roof to dry.'

Tanya raised her eyes to follow his pointing finger and suddenly it dawned on her that there was something very strange about the roof. There were not in fact three storeys at all, but two—only the roof was raised above the top of the house a good four metres, like a kind of canopy, giving the appearance of an additional floor. What she was looking at was a sort of ingenious raised drying green, open all sides to the winds, yet conveniently protected from the rain.

He dropped his arm and turned to her. 'I'll show you inside.'

She followed at a safe distance. With all the shutters closed the building would be dark inside, and though she knew beyond the slightest doubt that Fausto Cabrini was not the type of man to make grubby sexual overtures, she instinctively felt that the greater the distance she kept between the two of them the less vulnerable she would somehow be.

But, almost as though he had anticipated her thoughts, he crossed at once to the windows of the empty room he had led her into and pushed the shutters open wide. Then he leaned with his hips against the wooden windowsill, his dark head framed in bright sunlight, and gazed round at the bare floor and freshly plastered walls. 'As you can see, I've recently had the whole place converted. I plan to use it as a guest-house eventually. This will be the reception-room. Through there——' he nodded towards the door behind her '—is the kitchen. And there's a bathroom at the other side. Another bathroom and two bedrooms upstairs.' He pushed back the sleeves of his light blue shirt and folded his strong, tanned arms across his chest. 'So, Tanya, what do you think of it?'

It was the first time he had ever used her name and there was something oddly intimate about the gesture now. Almost as though he had reached out and touched her. She dropped her eyes hurriedly from his face. 'What am I supposed to think of it?' she countered half defensively.

'Whatever you please. But as a *designer* you must surely have some kind of opinion?' He stressed the word scornfully, apparently finding her claim to such a title quite ridiculous.

She resisted the urge to come back at him with some equally cutting barb of her own and instead answered coolly, matter-of-fact, 'It's a well proportioned room and it seems to get plenty of natural light. It could be nice.'

The dark-tanned face broke into an almost boyish grin. 'How very low key. I fear you will never succeed in selling your services if you insist on adopting that sort of approach.' Then, before she could point out to him that selling her services to him was actually the last thing on her mind, he moved away from the window and out into the hall again. 'Let's see if the upstairs rooms manage to fire you with a little more professional enthusiasm.'

He waited for her at the foot of the narrow, wooden staircase and stood aside to let her go ahead of him. She walked past him quickly, as though terrified that some part of their anatomies might accidentally touch, and almost sprinted up the stairs. The top landing was in darkness, and as he joined her there he leaned past her suddenly to switch on the light. She shrank back against the wall as for a moment it seemed as though his arm might brush against her breast. But he didn't touch her—though, as he smiled with what looked like mock-apology, he did seem dangerously close. 'I'm sorry, I should have switched the light on from downstairs. You might have tripped.'

She swallowed hard, hating herself for her discomfort, hating him even more for so obviously enjoying it. Then she breathed with relief as he moved away from her at last and pushed open one of the bedroom doors.

'This will be the master bedroom,' he explained, throwing open the shutters and turning round to look at her. 'The other one's slightly smaller. And the bathroom is situated between the two of them.' He waited, watching her. 'Well?'

'Well, what?'

'You tell me you're a designer. Do you think you can decorate this house for me?'

'Are you asking me?'

'Not exactly.'

'Telling me?'

He nodded. 'That's right.'

'But why would you want *me* to do it when you obviously have so little faith in my abilities?' That was something he had left her in no doubt about.

He shrugged. 'If you make a mess of it, I can simply rip the whole lot out and start again.' His voice carried an edge of almost calculated callousness. 'On the other hand, when you're lucky enough to have a designer in residence, it seems a bit silly not to make good use of her.'

This time Tanya could not resist the urge to pounce on him. 'You make a habit of using people, don't you? I've noticed it's something you like to mention quite a lot.'

'Of course.' He hooked his thumbs into the pockets of his linen trousers and looked across at her, quite unabashed. 'We all use each other, Tanya, whether we choose to admit it or not. We rely on each other's talents and abilities—even on each other's ambitions and aspirations to some extent. I use you. You use me. That's what makes the world go round.'

The black eyes held her tawny ones for a long moment, and the sense of unease that had steadily been growing inside Tanya since they had left the villa was suddenly almost unbearable. For some inexplicable reason, she felt trapped by this man. Cornered. As though by being in this place with him she was somehow putting herself at his mercy. It was ridiculous, of course, but no amount of telling herself that could change the way she felt. She forced herself to reply calmly, 'I would have expected a man like you to claim that it was money that made the world go round.'

'No, Tanya, money simply oils the wheels.' He regarded her for a moment longer, then remarked quite unexpectedly, 'Obviously you disagree. So what would you say makes the world go round?'

She might have said love, but she knew that he would only laugh at her. He had this ability to make everything she said sound both naïve and trivial. And she doubted very much in any case if he really had a clue about the meaning of the word. Love would not be a part of the sexual dimension he had spoken of. So she shrugged. 'You're the one with all the answers, not me.'

'Not all the answers—but enough to get by.' Then abruptly he straightened and started to walk towards the door. 'I'll just show you quickly round the roof.'

He led the way up a narrow iron staircase and pushed open the door at the top. 'Watch your feet,' he advised, stepping nimbly over the storm-step that separated the top of the staircase from the outside roof. Then, in a gesture that seemed totally spontaneous, he held out a helping hand to her. Equally spontaneously she accepted it—and his touch was like raw fire against her unsuspecting flesh. With a gasp almost of horror she quickly snatched her hand away.

He gave her a cool look and a hint of sardonic humour flashed in the dark eyes. 'I forgot. You don't need any help.'

'Not from you I don't!' she shot back, furious at her own craven response. Why did she find it so difficult to treat him with the contempt that he so fully deserved? What was it about the wretched man that so unsettled her whenever he was near?

He had crossed to the waist-high iron railing that enclosed the roof area, and as he moved a shaft of sunlight fell across his shoulders and half-clad arms. Involuntarily Tanya felt her eyes drawn to the bronzed and strongly muscled forearms that the rolled-back sleeves of his shirt revealed—and snatched them away as abruptly as she had snatched away her hand. He glanced at her over his shoulder. 'Of course, if you make a decent job of it, I'm quite prepared to pay you the going rate.'

Tanya sniffed. Trust him to waste no time in returning to the subject of money! And trust him also to make the assumption that her good will could be bought. 'If you're trying to fire my enthusiasm with bribes, forget it,' she answered him, bridling visibly. 'Unlike you, Signor Cabrini, financial reward has never been my primary motivation in life.'

He swivelled round to look at her. 'Then you're fortunate. That attitude is one that very few are able to afford. It is also, alas, the sort of attitude that lands people in all kinds of financial trouble. Then they have to rely on people like me to bail them out.' The allusion to her father was not hard to detect. If she wanted to trade insults, he clearly had no compunction about giving as good as he got. He added maliciously, 'And I don't remember you exactly turning up your nose back in Sussex when the big money was being handed out.'

Tanya's cheeks were burning with outraged anger

now. 'My interest in what went on that day was purely for my father's sake. In spite of the fact that you keep on insisting otherwise, I had no personal stake in the proceedings at all. Not everyone is driven by the narrow self-interest that so obviously drives you.'

He ignored her taunt and came straight back on the attack instead. 'You're trying to tell me that if your father went under financially it would make no personal difference to you? Wouldn't you rather miss the easy, comfortable life-style he's always given you? Wouldn't you find it rather difficult to give up all the little luxuries?' Scorn dripped from his every syllable. 'I find your protests difficult to swallow, I'm afraid.'

'Well, you're wrong!' Why was he always attacking her? 'Of course I'd miss all these things you mention. I'm not going to deny that. But it wouldn't be the end of the world for me. I'm still young enough and fit enough to make my own way in life——'

'To find another man to keep you, you mean,' he cut in cruelly, the dark eyes sending a bitter challenge across the narrow distance that divided them.

'That isn't what I mean at all!' If she had been a man, she would have struck him then. 'What I mean is, if my father went broke, it would be a tragedy for him, but not for me. He would never recover. I could. And, all along—whether you want to believe it or not—it's my father that I've been worried about.' And she knew it was the truth, in spite of him.

'Well, well. You're all heart, aren't you?'

'At least I'm human, with human feelings, which is more than you appear to be.'

'You're one of life's takers, Tanya, that's what you are. That's why I'm going to take such pleasure in squeezing every last drop of hard work out of you. You'll learn how it feels to contribute for once. I'm going to teach you what it means to pull your weight.'

She was boiling inside. One more word from him and she would explode. 'I've already heard your threats!' she stormed at him, the words spitting from her lips like poisoned darts.

They were mere pinpricks. He smiled. 'And listened to them well, I hope.'

She glared at him, hardly trusting herself to speak.

'To return to specifics, I'd like you to start work on the wash-house as soon as possible. Since the money that I offered doesn't interest you, you will no doubt be eager to get started for your father's sake. But, whatever your motivations, you'll have plenty of time. I won't be needing you in the office all day every day.' His tone was as hard and unyielding as the expression on his face. He paused. 'Which reminds me—did you sort things out with your relatives in Austria?'

'I phoned them as you instructed me.' And had explained, without going into any of the reasons why, that she would not be able to spend the summer with them, after all.

'And your father? Did you call the clinic to let him know you're here?'

'I did.' Perhaps, she was beginning to think, she should have submitted a written report.

'Did you also tell him why?' He had stepped forward and was standing almost right in front of her, hands thrust in his trouser pockets.

'Of course not!' She thrust her own hands into the pockets of her slim white skirt, deliberately facing up to him. 'I think my father's health is already quite precarious enough without confronting him with that sort of bad news over the telephone. I intend to tell him about the icon next time I see him. There isn't any rush, is there?' Her stomach was churning with anger now.

'No rush. I have you here with me, after all, to take the icon's place.' He smiled at her briefly, a harsh and humourless smile, then glanced down quickly at his watch. 'I have to get back to the office now. I suggest you stay and have a closer look round here.' He started to move away.

Suddenly Tanya could no longer contain the rage and frustration that were bubbling inside. She turned on him. 'This whole situation is ridiculous, you know! You can't keep me here against my will! What if I just decide to go? What if I just get on a plane and fly back to England and to hell with you? There isn't a damned thing you could do about it!' She flung the challenge at him like a physical assault—then clenched her fists tightly at her sides and waited for him to retaliate.

His response came at her with the speed and the force of a shot from a gun. 'I wouldn't do that if I were you. Stamping your feet and demanding your own way isn't going to get you anywhere for once.' A fire of anger more than equal to her own blazed in the dark eyes. 'Take my word for it, you'd be well advised just to do exactly as I say.'

But she would not let go. Like a Pekinese snapping at a stallion's heels, she started to follow him to the door. 'You don't scare me! What could you do if I refused to stay? Destroy my father? Withdraw the loan? You may be a bastard, but I can't believe that even you are quite as big a bastard as all that!'

He swung round on her then, his face pale with fury beneath the darkness of his tan. 'Don't push me, Tanya, I'm warning you. You'll only be sorry if you do. And don't try to run out on me either—not unless you want to see me bring your father to his knees. For, believe me, I'd do it without a second thought.' He fixed her with a vicious look. 'If you want to find out if I'm serious or not, just try me.'

She stepped back, suddenly chilled by the appalling certainty that he meant every heartless word he said.

The cruel message in the deep, dark eyes left her in no doubt of that. Her tongue felt like cold clay in her mouth. There seemed to be nothing left for her to say.

Half-stunned, she watched as he stepped out through the door, then paused to deliver his parting shot. 'Be ready to leave at seven-thirty sharp for our dinner appointment in Milan.' He cast a scathing glance in the direction of her feet. 'And do me the favour of removing your shoes on your journey back to the villa, please. I prefer my escorts not to have their feet covered in sticking plaster.'

He was gone before she could reply—with the last word as usual, she fumed.

The front door slammed and she peered down on a fresh wave of resentment to see Fausto Cabrini emerge from the house and quickly cross the little clearing back to the wood. Again that uneasy voice of warning stirred deep in her soul. Make no mistake, it seemed to be telling her—beware! This man is capable of inflicting the most deadly wounds.

CHAPTER FOUR

AFTER Cabrini had gone, Tanya quite happily spent the rest of the afternoon exploring the old wash-house and its surroundings more thoroughly. One thing was for sure, the designers who had converted the old building had done an inspired job. By the time she finally closed the front door some hours later, her head was buzzing with ideas. Within the next two weeks, she promised herself, she would sketch out a few of those ideas for Cabrini to approve.

Tanya got back to the villa about half past five. The aquamarine dress was hanging, neatly pressed, from the door of the wardrobe in her room and Emma had placed a big vase of fresh flowers on the little table by the window. Gratefully Tanya sank down on the bed and stretched her arms above her head. All the walking she had done, plus the early start and the general excitement of the day, had tired her out. She would close her eyes and rest for a couple of minutes, she decided, before running a bath and starting to get ready for the evening ahead. Half past seven, Cabrini had said. She had loads of time.

The next thing she knew the telephone was ringing in her ear and she sat up with a start. The room had grown dark. My God, she thought in sudden panic, what time is it? She groped for the blue phone, somehow guessing who would be on the other end, and spoke into it as brightly as she could, praying he wouldn't be able to detect the husky tones of sleep still in her voice.

'I'm sorry to disturb you.' She had been right, it was Fausto Cabrini's cool, sarcastic tones that answered her.

'I hope I didn't get you out of the shower this time.' She pulled a wry face to herself. If only he knew the truth— that she had been sound asleep! 'I'm afraid I'm not going to be ready for half past seven,' he went on. 'I seem to have been tied up on the telephone all afternoon and I'm going to need another quarter of an hour.' He paused.

'Oh, that's all right,' she assured him, desperately groping for the light switch so that she could see what time it was.

'I'll meet you downstairs at a quarter to eight. Just help yourself to a drink while you're waiting.'

Fat chance of that! She put the phone down and succeeded at last in locating the button on the bedside lamp. Squinting anxiously at her watch, she saw with mingled horror and relief that it was ten past seven. That gave her just over half an hour to shower—no time for a bath now—wash and dry her hair, put on her make-up and get dressed. The last thing she wanted was to keep the great Fausto Cabrini waiting again. It had taken her long enough to live that first time down!

He was waiting for her in the hall as she came down the stairs—wearing a dark suit that somehow emphasised the breadth of his shoulders, and a fine, white silk shirt that flattered the sun-bronzed features beneath the smooth sweep of thick, black hair. He smiled, the dark eyes openly appraising as she descended. 'It suits you,' was all he said—but the real compliment could be read in his expression rather than in the words he spoke.

Tanya felt a faint blush stain her cheeks. The dress did wonders for her, there was no doubt about that. Its elegant cut—softly draped over the bust, moulded to fit around the waist and hips—dramatically accentuated her naturally slim shapeliness, and the colour provided a perfect foil for her creamy complexion and golden hair. But Fausto Cabrini's approval was something she very definitely did not need. She raised her eyebrows haughtily and glanced down at him from the height advantage of the last few stairs. 'So glad you approve,' she murmured with a less than subtle twist of sarcasm in her voice.

His eyes swept downwards to her cream-slippered feet and paused in pointed scrutiny. 'No sticking plaster, I see.' The corners of his well shaped mouth lifted in an openly amused, sardonic little smile. 'I'm surprised you can walk after the punishment you inflicted on them this afternoon. You really should have taken my advice.' The black eyes seemed to challenge her.

That'll be the day! was her instantaneous response, but she refrained from expressing the sentiment out loud. Instead, she glided past him with all the disdain she could muster and retorted coolly, 'Signor Cabrini, I do assure you I really am perfectly capable of looking after myself—including my feet.' Which wasn't altogether accurate, she acknowledged ruefully to herself. After this afternoon's ordeal her feet were feeling decidedly tender in places. She would just have to keep her fingers crossed that she wouldn't be required to walk any great distances tonight.

'I'm glad to hear it,' he responded mockingly. 'As I've already told you, I've no desire to end up having to carry you.' Then he broke off and very deliberately held her eyes. 'My name is Fausto, by the way. Much less cumbersome than "Signor Cabrini", don't you think?' And he quickly walked past her to the door. 'Now I suggest that we be on our way. Our table is booked for half past eight and we really ought to arrive ahead of our guests.'

A sleek white Lamborghini was parked and waiting for them in the forecourt, the keys in the ignition, and Tanya wondered idly just how many cars Fausto Cabrini possessed. He pulled open the passenger door for her and she climbed inside. 'You may find it a bit low,' he observed as she sat down, straightening the skirt of her dress. 'It's not the easiest car in the world to get in and out of elegantly, but at least it's fast.'

And that, Tanya observed drily to herself as they were storming down the *autostrada* less than fifteen minutes later, must be the understatement of the year. He drove with the same cool confidence as he seemed to do everything else. The grip of the long, tanned fingers on the steering-wheel was light yet spoke of absolute authority, like the firm, sure touch of an experienced rider on the reins of his mount. And, like the experienced rider, Tanya felt instinctively, he knew precisely how to coax and control this powerful mechanical beast to do his bidding. He was its master. In spite of the hair-raising speed they were travelling at, she felt no fear, only an unexpected sense of exhilaration.

He slowed down as the traffic on the *autostrada* began to thicken a few kilometres outside Milan, and addressed her without taking his eyes from the road. 'You've spent some time in Milan. Perhaps you know the Ristorante La Traviata where we're going tonight.'

She shook her head. She had heard of it, of course—it was one of the most exclusive and expensive restaurants in Milan—but she had never actually eaten there. 'By reputation only, I'm afraid. I didn't stay in Milan as long as I would have liked. Only for about six months as it turned out—and there are a lot of places I would like to have seen that I never got round to visiting.'

'I would have thought the social sights would have been the first priority for a girl like you.'

Angrily she swivelled round to glare at him. 'My studies were my first priority.' Why was he always so quick to label her as shallow and frivolous? 'It was a great disappointment to me when I had to leave.'

'So what's to stop you picking up where you left off?'

If only she could! The interior design diploma from the Accademia in Milan would be a valuable qualification, she knew. But she had few hopes of returning to complete her final year in the forseeable future, now that Devlin was so ill and likely to need her by his side. 'Maybe I shall one of these days,' she answered quietly.

They were coming up to the final toll station before turning off the *autostrada* and heading for the centre of Milan, and suddenly the dark interior of the car was flooded with light. Cabrini turned to look at her as they joined the line of cars at one of the half-dozen pay booths straddling the road and the black eyes beneath the strongly arched brows held a strange expression she had never seen in them before.

'I'm sorry if I was out of line back there,' he said. 'Renata told me how you gave up your studies when your mother died. I'd forgotten. I should never have brought the subject up.'

His apology took her totally by surprise. 'Don't worry,' she assured him quickly, dropping her eyes and turning away from the dark, penetrating gaze that was suddenly quite unsettling. 'I don't mind you mentioning it. It doesn't upset me to talk about my mother.' She sighed lightly as an image of the passionate and vital woman who had filled her childhood with so much love and happiness flitted across her mind. 'Of course, I miss her very much, but I have so many happy memories of her to treasure. In a way, she will always be alive for me.' She shook her head. 'The real tragedy when she died was for my father. They were devoted to one another. Sometimes I wonder if he will ever recover from her death.'

They passed through the toll and Cabrini headed for the sliproad that would take them to the centre of the city. For a minute or two he said nothing, then when he spoke there was an odd note of detachment in his voice, as though he were talking to himself as much as her. 'It's sad, of course, but in a way I envy your father. It must be a wonderful thing to have a marriage like that.' He paused. 'And you, Tanya, should consider yourself lucky, too. To grow up in a home where there is so much love is a very rare and special thing.'

A strange sensation tugged at Tanya as she glanced now at the hard features etched in darkness against the sodium lights. Could it be that she had just glimpsed a softer, more vulnerable side to the man? He had spoken then with an unguarded candour quite out of character with the arrogant self-possession with which he generally confronted the world. Could it be that the man had a heart, was prey to ordinary human feelings, after all? No, what she had glimpsed then was a mere momentary lapse of no significance, she decided, discounting out of hand the very possibility. It would be sheer whimsy on her part to suspect otherwise.

They reached the restaurant just a few minutes before their guests. Cabrini rose politely to his feet as the two middle-aged couples approached their table—the men sleek and prosperous-looking, their wives immaculately and expensively groomed—and Tanya felt a quick surge of gratitude that she was wearing Renata's aquamarine dress. In anything less elegant she would have felt completely out of place.

The four took their seats in a flurry of distinguished *bonhomie* and expensive French scent. Aperitifs were ordered, introductions made. Mario and Carla Alfonsi, it appeared to Tanya, were typical examples of the Italian *alta borghesia*, he with his trim moustache and Savile Row dinner-jacket, she with her faultless beauty-parlour complexion and discreet pearl choker glowing at her neck. The Banuccis appeared to have been cast from a slightly different mould. Giorgio, in spite of the hand-cut cashmere and silk he wore, had a rougher, earthier edge to him that Tanya somehow found reassuring, and Gabriella, though garbed and coiffed as elegantly as Carla, seemed less precariously poised on her dignity than the other woman.

And, in fact, it was Gabriella who made the first conversational overture to Tanya as they laid aside their menus and waited for the *antipasti* to arrive. 'Fausto tells me you really saved his bacon by stepping in at the last minute when his other secretary let him down. I'm sure a pretty girl like you had better things to do than slave away over a hot typewriter all summer long.'

Tanya was aware of dark eyes watching her from across the table as she made her response. 'Oh, not at all,' she answered brightly, wondering at her own enthusiasm. 'I was at a loose end, actually. I was quite delighted when Signor—eh, Fausto—invited me to fill in for a few months.'

With a look of defiance, she met the dark gaze. A flicker of amusement briefly curled the corners of his lips. 'Of course, Tanya is a good friend of Renata's,' he very pointedly informed the table at large. 'In fact, a good friend of the family, really, you could say. Isn't that right, Tanya?'

She was saved from having to perjure herself by an innocent exclamation from Gabriella. 'How lovely! So you're a friend of Renata's—I didn't realise. What a charming girl Renata is.'

On that point, at least, she could agree with total sincerity. And resisted the temptation to add, 'And so totally unlike her brother.'

'You must feel quite at home, then, at the Villa Cabrini,' Gabriella pursued enthusiastically. 'That's nice. It's so much more pleasant to be among friends in a foreign land.'

Tanya exchanged a brief, ironic glance with the dark-suited figure seated opposite and let the ill-judged observation pass. With friends like Fausto Cabrini, who needed enemies?

In time the conversation moved on to weightier matters of business, and for the most part Tanya found herself a mere observer, but, nevertheless, a fascinated one. The talk of base rates and MLR and Euro-currency deposits passed largely uncomprehended over her head, but watching the five participants was an entertainment in itself.

There was never a moment of doubt about who the star of the show might be, but Tanya had to admit, albeit rather reluctantly, that Cabrini was a deft performer. He knew how to share the limelight, encouraging the others to play their parts. He knew when to step into the background and when to move forward on to centre stage. His timing was impeccable. And his four co-stars seemed as happily involved in the performance as he appeared to be.

It was perfectly obvious they all held their host in the greatest respect, and, grudgingly, Tanya found it not too difficult to appreciate why. He had the air of a man who knew what he was talking about, whose aura of profound authority and dominance was founded on more than just a deep sense of personal superiority—for that was part of his power, too. More important, though, he radiated expertise, a complete mastery of the business he dealt in. And, for that, Tanya felt a sneaking admiration. Even respect.

It was well into the evening when the woman with the bright blonde hair and purple silk catsuit suddenly appeared. Tanya saw her from across the room as she swept between the crowded tables on the arm of her escort, looking as though she owned the place. And for a brief moment the eyes of the two women met—though it was more of a clash than a meeting, Tanya acknowl-edged to herself in puzzlement. A moment later the woman was standing at Fausto Cabrini's elbow, her escort having conveniently melted into the crowd, and Tanya wasn't feeling puzzled any more.

She was obviously one of his women, Tanya surmised, observing the proprietary hand that gripped his arm as the blonde head bent to kiss him lingeringly on each cheek. '*Fausto, caro! Che piacere incontrarti.* How lovely bumping into you.' She was in her mid-thirties, Tanya guessed. A bit on the loud side, but attractive enough if you happened to like that sort of thing.

Fausto Cabrini apparently did. He smiled and lightly encircled the purple silk waist with one arm as he responded, with easy, familiar charm, to the woman's overtures. And Tanya watched with mingled fascination and distaste as the fond creature fluttered and giggled, like a woman half her age, at every charming and witty thing he said. Whoever she was, she must have been born with about as much perception as a loaf of bread!

The woman was quite clearly already acquainted with the Alfonsis and the Banuccis, though she dispensed no more than a cursory nod to each of them. It was indubitably Fausto that she had crossed the restaurant to see—though Tanya was aware that she cast more than one glance in her own direction, a curiously cautionary expression in the wide green eyes. The presence of the young girl in the aquamarine dress at Cabrini's table was obviously troubling her. There was an element almost of belligerence in the way she so undisguisedly was wondering who Tanya was.

She was still wondering ten minutes later as she prepared to take her leave. Cabrini had not introduced the two of them—a deliberate omission, Tanya felt. The woman cast a bright smile round the table. 'So sorry to interrupt you, *signore e signori,*' she declared in an oddly condescending tone of voice. 'I'll leave you to get on with your dinner and your conversation now.'

'No need to apologise, *contessa*. A pleasure to see you.'
This was accompanied by a gallant inclination of the
head from Giorgio—for which he was rewarded with a
dazzling smile.

So she was a countess. Evidently the Italian aristoc-
racy was on the slide. Tanya eyed her with bitchy
disapproval as she bent once more to embrace Cabrini.
'*A presto, caro.* I'll see you soon.'

He acknowledged her entreaty with another charming smile. '*A presto. Stai bene.* Look after yourself.'

Then, plucking her hand almost reluctantly from
Fausto Cabrini's sleeve, she started at last to move away,
but not before pausing to deliver a final warning glance
at Tanya. If looks could kill, Tanya found herself
pondering with a quiet smile. The countess was
definitely one friend that she hadn't made tonight.

And later, when the little dinner party finally broke
up, she was aware of a pair of dark green eyes boring into
the back of her skull as she followed Cabrini to the
door—and with difficulty resisted the urge to turn
around. If some silly woman of Fausto Cabrini's was
suffering pangs of jealousy because of her, the last thing
she wanted was to get involved. She had enough
problems of her own, thank you. Let them keep their
nasty little affair to themselves.

But, in spite of all that, she was feeling oddly elated as
she settled back into the soft contours of the Lamborghini's passenger seat, and she even permitted herself
a relaxed, almost contented sigh as Fausto climbed into
the driver's seat beside her.

'I hope you didn't find all that too boring,' he said,
gunning the engine and heading back in the direction of
the *autostrada*.

'Not in the least,' Tanya informed him lazily as she
leaned back and watched the city lights flash by. 'As a

matter of fact, I found the whole thing rather illuminating.'

'Did you now?' The big car gave a throaty growl as he changed down the gears and headed up the slipway to the toll gates. 'And which particular aspects of the proceedings, Tanya, did you find of special note?'

Tanya straightened slightly in her seat, a fleeting irritation pursing her lips as she prepared to answer him. Did he never relax? Did he have to cross-examine her at every turn? 'It was interesting to see how you do business. To see how you manipulate your clients,' she added spitefully, reluctant to heap praise.

But he only turned and smiled at her under the bright arc-lights of the toll station. An amused smile, superior and confident. Like the man himself, she reflected drily, avoiding the dark eyes. He already knew how good he was. He certainly didn't need her to tell him. 'And how do I manipulate my clients, Tanya? Elaborate.'

'Most cleverly. I doubt they even realise they're being manipulated.'

He laughed out loud then. 'That goes without saying. Manipulation, to be effective, must be subtle. As a woman, that is something you must surely know.'

She decided to ignore that last, sexist remark. The evening had been pleasant and, for once, she was in no mood for a fight. Half closing her eyes, she relaxed back against the deep, soft leather of her seat, enjoying again the quick thrill of exitement as the big car surged away from the bright lights of the toll station, heading for the darkened fast lane of the *autostrada*.

It was a strange excitement, this sensation of power. The power of the machine, fierce and fragile, that hurtled them with apparent effortlessness through the night. And the power of the man beside her that controlled it. For, above all, it was the power of the man she felt—unyielding, ruthlessly cruel and irresistible. It was a power that both drew and repelled her at the same time, that stirred some basic animal passion of her own deep within, that would hold her captive in its seductive thrall if she only dared give in to it. But she did not dare.

Abruptly, she snapped her eyes open. Was she taking leave of her senses?

'I thought you'd fallen asleep.'

She glanced quickly at the dark, aquiline profile, then, just as quickly, glanced away again. 'Just thinking.' But what thoughts!

'Weren't you going to enlighten me with your observations on the proceedings tonight?' His tone held that familiar, mocking ring.

'If you like.'

'I like. The intuitive female interpretation always interests me.'

Instinctively Tanya felt her hackles rise. From the lips of a man like Fausto Cabrini, intuitive could only be a slur. A male chauvinist euphemism for irrational. She squared her shoulders and stared straight ahead. 'Well, I think I've figured out why you like to meet your clients with their wives.'

'Do tell.'

She ignored the note of condescension in his voice and carried on. 'Well, apart from the fact that it undoubtedly flatters your male ego to have those wealthy Milanese matrons sighing at your every syllable, I can see that their presence serves a purpose of sorts. Not so much in the case of the Alfonsis, of course. Mario Alfonsi appears to be so smitten by your financial prowess that he would go along with virtually anything you said. And his wife couldn't care less how her husband's money is invested, just so long as the profits keep her in pearl chokers and face-lifts for the next thirty years. I suspect she's happy to tag along just to keep an eye on her husband as much as anything.'

He gave a low laugh. 'Neatly observed. Continue. What about the Banuccis? What did you make of them?'

'Those two are a totally different kettle of fish,' Tanya went on, warming to her analysis. 'Giorgio strikes me as an impulsive, impatient sort of guy. He wants every nickel and dime explained to him and justified. He wants to see quick profits. Short-term results in favour of investments that might possibly yield more favourably in the longer term. And that, of course, is where Gabriella comes in. She's the more level-headed of the two, she's not in such a hurry as her husband. I doubt if she would ever oppose her husband in public, of course, but I'd bet that once they get home she'll persuade him round to your way of thinking with no trouble at all. I could see her taking mental notes of everything you said while you and her husband were arguing over the *bocchini di vitello*. Gabriella is your back-up system when it comes to dealing with Giorgio.'

'Clever girl!' His hand reached out briefly and patted her knee. Automatically, she winced away. 'I had no idea you were such an astute observer, Tanya. I can see that you and I are going to make a perfect team. Your predecessor wasn't half as smart as you.'

'Is that why you fired her?' The question was out before she could stop herself. Perversely, his praise had irritated rather than pleased her. And her knee was still tingling where he had touched her. That annoyed her too.

'I didn't fire her, as a matter of fact. She left.' There was a hard, cold edge to his voice that told her their conversation was at an end. They drove the rest of the way to the lake in chilly silence, and Tanya was relieved when they swept at last through the tall iron portals into the grounds of the Cabrini estate.

By the time they reached the villa, however, he appeared to have recovered from his flash of ill-humour.

'I suggest a nightcap.' He motioned her through the hall to the drawing-room, evidently taking her acquiescence for granted. 'I find a drop of brandy helps me to relax after a busy day.'

Tanya would rather have gone straight to bed, but she felt it ill-advised to make a fuss. Better to end the evening on an agreeable note, she decided. And one little brandy couldn't hurt.

It was a big, stately room that by day looked out over the terrace to the lawns and flowerbeds and the lake beneath. Now, the heavy silk brocade curtains were drawn and low, silk-shaded table-lamps cast a soft illumination over lustrous, rose-coloured silk-hung walls. The room was furnished with a mix of deep, comfortable modern sofas and warm, well-loved-looking antiques. Tanya settled herself against the cushions of a voluminous wing-backed armchair and watched as he poured two generous measures from a bottle of Remy Martin. Then he warmed the two balloons in the palms of his hands before handing her one.

He slipped off his jacket and flung it casually over the back of the nearest sofa before seating himself with a sigh in the armchair next to her. 'Well, that's your first day in,' he commented, taking a long, slow mouthful from his glass, then rolling the fiery liquid round in his mouth for a moment before finally swallowing it. 'I hope I haven't tired you out.'

'Not at all. I'm quite used to working long hours—in spite of what you seem to think.'

'Is that so?' The dark head inclined at an angle as he surveyed her through amused black eyes. The strongly chiselled features, that could appear harsh and uncompromising in some lights, were somehow softened in the pale glow of the silk-clad lamps. The finely moulded mouth curved in a smile. 'Well, you definitely will be when I'm through with you.'

She threw him a caustic look. 'God, you really like to gloat. Do you have to keep rubbing it in *all* the time?'

If the shot was intended to rebuke, it missed its mark. He continued to smile at her unrepentantly. 'So what shall we talk about instead? Eh, Tanya? Pick a subject. You're in charge.'

The irony was hardly lost on her. She had seldom felt less in charge in her entire life. She kicked the cream leather pumps from her feet and curled her long, slender legs up under her.

'Feet hurting?' he enquired wickedly.

'Not a bit,' she shot back, not quite truthfully.

'I'm glad to hear it.' Again he smiled.

It was infuriating the way he always seemed to have the upper hand with her. Alone in his presence she felt gauche, uncertain of herself and vulnerable. And there was no logic to it. She loathed the man, detested him, and yet he seemed to wield an uncanny sort of power over her, a power that scared and thrilled her at the same time, yet a power she was utterly determined to resist.

He was still watching her, long legs stretched out easily in front of him, his tie now discarded and the top few buttons of his shirt undone, exposing a tantalising triangle of powerful, sun-darkened chest. Broad shoulders moved sinuously against thin silk as he rolled the cognac contemplatively around in his glass. He seemed to be waiting for her to speak.

Tanya took a quick mouthful of her drink and felt the liquid burn a trail of fire to her stomach. He continued to wait. The silence between them was beginning to unnerve her slightly. She pillaged her brain for something inconsequential to say—and found it. 'Have you lived here long?' she asked, and cringed inwardly. Well, you couldn't get more trite than that!

He smiled a small smile, sensing her unease, no doubt.

'Since I bought it—almost seven years ago.'

'*Bought* it?' she responded, taken by surprise. 'But I thought it had been in your family for generations.'

He threw back his head at that and laughed, a rich, deep laugh of genuine amusement. 'Not at all, Tanya. Don't let the coincidence of name mislead you. The Barons Cabrini who owned this estate for centuries were no relatives of mine. Unlike you, I have not a drop of blue blood flowing through my veins.' And he paused as her cheeks flushed at his words. 'Renata told me of your noble lineage.'

Tanya shifted defensively in her chair, uncertain whether he was making fun of her or not. 'They were only very minor members of the Russian nobility. Not exactly Romanovs.'

But the dark eyes that met hers for once held not a trace of mockery. 'You should be proud of them. They were your mother's family.' He smoothed his dark hair with one hand. 'My forebears were poor Italian peasants—until my grandparents emigrated to the United States. Strange, isn't it, how history shapes the destiny of the individual? Your grandparents were forced to flee from the country of their birth because of a revolution, mine because of poverty.'

She waited as he smiled a low, wry smile and drained his glass—and secretly hoped that he would go on. In spite of the antipathy she felt for him, she was curious to know more about the man.

He smiled as though he were reading her mind. 'The land of opportunity, that's where they went. And my old grandfather grabbed every opportunity that was going with both hands. Within a generation he'd built the foundations of a thriving little industrial empire. Farm machinery—that was what he started with—then radios, refrigerators. It was all very basic and unsophisticated at the time, of course, but it made him a fortune all the same.

'Then my father came along and moved into electronics at just the right time. When my grandfather died, just over twenty years ago, my father decided to move the bulk of the family's interests back to Italy. Milan. In some ways he was a bit of a romantic, my father. Though not in others. Certainly not as far as his wife and children were concerned.'

He paused and gazed into his empty glass, and Tanya watched him without saying a word. Just for a moment then, with that almost resentful reference to this father, he had seemed to let his iron-clad defences down. For an instant, he had appeared before her naked, vulnerable, human. But, as though it had never happened, the moment passed. 'I was about fourteen years old when my father returned to Italy,' he continued, totally composed again. 'Renata and I remained in the States with our mother. She was a third-generation New Yorker with absolutely nothing to bring her to Milan—certainly not my father. Then when she died ten years ago, I came over to join my father. It was curiosity as much as anything, I suppose—or maybe I'm a bit of a romantic too.' He shot her a smile that warned her not to take that last remark too literally. Not that she was in any danger of doing that.

'As it turned out I discovered that I liked it here. I decided to settle. Then when I heard that old Baron Cabrini had died and his estate on Lake Maggiore was up for sale, I decided to buy it. My great-great-grandmother once worked as a washerwoman on the estate. Let's just say the irony appealed to me.'

There was a short silence, then Tanya ventured quietly, 'So the conversion of the old wash-house must have a special meaning for you.'

'I suppose it does.' Cabrini laid down his empty glass

and ran his fingers through his thick, dark hair. 'But we've talked enough for tonight, Tanya. Time for bed.'

She sighed, suddenly realising how tired she was. She got to her feet with a guarded glance at the seated figure just a matter of inches away. For some reason his revelations had left her feeling even more confused. The monster had assumed a face. No longer the arrogant automaton she had believed he was. From now on, he would not be quite so easy to hate. The knowledge disturbed her.

He had risen from his chair and was watching her. 'What are you waiting for, Tanya?'

'Nothing.' She wanted to move away, but still she hesitated. His nearness, the raw male power of him seemed to hypnotise. She wanted to say something to break the spell, but could not think what. She felt foolish, helpless, utterly appalled at herself. But still she could not move away.

Then it was too late. He reached out and grabbed her roughly by the arm, pulling her to him in a vice-like grip so that she felt the hard length of his lean, male body pressing against her. 'Is this what you were waiting for, Tanya?' he demanded gruffly as his mouth sought hers, his free arm clamping firmly round her waist as she sought belatedly to back away. Her feeble gasp of protest then was lost in the thrilling savagery of his kiss. A kiss that was hard, demanding, masterful, stunning her senses, sending bittersweet shockwaves of excitement coursing through her body.

Still she wanted to pull away, but she could not. And it was not just the hard, constraining strength of him that held her there. Some treacherous demon inside herself was urging her achingly to submit to his assault. And more than just submit. Respond. Then as his mouth began to force her lips apart so that he could deepen his kiss, a sudden panic gave her strength. But he released her almost before she started to pull away.

Her limbs were trembling and her hand flew to cover her bruised and swollen mouth. 'You bastard!' she spat. 'You had no right to do that!'

The dark eyes were cool, expressionless. No sign of the passion that had raged there just a moment ago. His lips curved in a cruel, sardonic smile. 'I suggest you go to bed now, Tanya. Unless you want more.'

Speechless with fury she turned and stumbled for the door.

'Goodnight,' he called after her on a mocking note. 'Sweet dreams.'

CHAPTER FIVE

TANYA scarcely slept at all that night and the dreams that tormented her when she finally did manage to drop off, shortly before dawn, were far from sweet.

The events of the previous evening haunted her. It had all started out so civilly. The dinner with Cabrini's clients in Milan had been entertaining and enjoyable, the only jarring note the brief appearance of the blonde woman in the purple catsuit. And that had had nothing to do with her! The drive back—apart from that brief lapse when she had unwisely raised the subject of his former secretary—had been pleasant enough. Even their conversation over brandy in the drawing-room, for once, had been perfectly harmonious. So why had everything suddenly gone wrong? Unless, of course, she told herself suspiciously, he had planned that little seduction scene right from the start.

But immediately she brushed aside the idea as absurd. What had happened last night could hardly be described as seduction. A physical assault, more like. A punishment. There had been no tenderness whatsoever in his kiss, just raw, animal aggression—and afterwards, when he had let her go, only cool, amused contempt in the dark eyes. It was almost as though he had been trying to teach her a lesson. And certainly not a lesson in love.

And she shuddered and felt herself colour at the memory. For the most disturbing part of all of it, the part she could only barely bring herself to recognise, was that she had actually wanted him to kiss her—and to go on kissing her. And shame swept through her as she recalled what clamour of sensations that kiss of his had

87

aroused in her. Sensations she had never experienced before. Strange sensations that had scared her with their raw intensity, stampeding aside all reason, stripping her soul, inflaming a hunger she knew she could never dare to satisfy.

She awoke the following morning with one certain resolution in her mind—that what had happened the night before must never, never happen again. Nothing in her past experience had equipped her to cope with anything like this. Sexually, she was a near-total innocent. The relationships she had known had been little more than friendships, safe and unthreatening. Fausto Cabrini, she knew with total certainty, was in an altogether different league.

As luck would have it, she didn't even set eyes on him that day till after lunch. She arrived at her desk at eight that morning to find a pile of letters and reports to type, along with a warning note that he would be tied up on the phone for the next few hours and did not wish to be disturbed. Be grateful for small mercies, she told herself with a sigh of relief as she settled down at her typewriter.

Around quarter to one, just as she was beginning to wonder about the arrangements for lunch, he buzzed through to her office. 'I'm waiting for a call from Kuwait,' he told her in a detached and businesslike tone of voice. 'Feel free to have lunch whenever you want. Emma will have something prepared.'

So lunch together on the terrace, she was extremely relieved to learn, was not going to be a regular affair. Though she should have known, of course. Fausto Cabrini was not a man to do things by numbers or follow any strict routine. He had already demonstrated that pretty conclusively.

Emma had indeed prepared something for lunch—a delicious *sformato di legumi*, a sort of super-sophisticated soufflé stuffed with mushrooms and tomatoes and aubergines. Tanya gulped it down hungrily—all this hard work was giving her an appetite! Then she settled back with a tiny cup of thick, black espresso to survey her surroundings with tranquillity.

The enormous terrace where she sat ran the entire length of the villa, with doors opening on to it from both the dining-room and the sitting-room. Tubs of riotous geraniums in every shade of red and pink were spaced along the waist-high parapet, drawing the eye outwards over the immaculate lawns and down through the trees towards the lake. Tanya sighed as she drank in the heady spectacle of it all. It was perfect. Well, almost.

A tall, lean figure in a blue tracksuit had suddenly appeared at the far end of the lawn beside the trees and was jogging now across the grass towards the terrace. Tanya had no need to look twice. She would recognise that figure anywhere. She gulped back her coffee and debated whether or not to exit hastily, but decided reluctantly to stay. He was so close now that he had almost certainly seen her, and she had no desire to make herself look like an idiot. So she sat tight, feigning nonchalance and silently cursing herself for not having noticed him before.

He came up the stone steps to the terrace two at a time and paused at the top to grin at her. The dark hair was ruffled and a fine film of sweat shone on his brow. She felt an involuntary quickening in the pit of her stomach at the sight of him, suppressed it instantly and shaded her eyes with one hand as she somewhat self-consciously returned his smile. 'That looks like a rather energetic way to spend your lunch hour,' she observed.

'You should try it some time, Tanya. There's nothing like a bit of physical exercise for sharpening the mind.'

In which case, Tanya observed without humour to herself, he had little need of exercise. His mind was already more than adequately sharp.

He crossed the space between them in a couple of
strides and, without waiting to be invited, lowered his
muscular frame into the vacant chair at Tanya's side.
'I've been meaning to give you these.' He pulled what
looked like a set of car keys from his tracksuit pocket and
laid them on the table in front of her. 'The blue Alfa. It's
in the garage at the back of the villa. Feel free to use it
whenever you like.' He leaned back and smiled a
tantalising smile. 'I wouldn't like you to feel you were
being treated like a prisoner.'

Tanya threw him a withering glance. 'What's the
matter? Is your conscience bothering you?'

He ran one sun-browned hand over his hair. 'I have
no conscience, Tanya. I thought that was something you
would have realised by now.' There was taunting
amusement in his eyes.

She gave a dismissive little shrug. 'I confess I
wouldn't find that terribly difficult to believe. But your
conscience, or the lack of it, like everything else about
you, I'm afraid, is really not of the slightest interest to
me.'

'Really?'

'Yes, really.'

He was sitting far too close to her, not touching, yet
distractingly near enough to touch. And she was
suddenly uncomfortably aware of the hard male contours of his body beneath the thin tracksuit—and her
body burned again, remembering that shameful kiss.
She swallowed, aware that her throat had suddenly gone
dry.

'Then why are you so curious to know about my
secretary?' he said. 'Why did you go to the trouble of
asking Emma why she left?'

Tanya felt herself blanch and hastily lowered her eyes
from the disturbing dark gaze. She had been right to
consider that exercise for the sake of sharpening his

mind was really quite superfluous. The wretched man was capable of figuring out far more than was good for him. Or her. 'What makes you think I did?' she bluffed.

'I know you did.'

'Emma told you, I suppose.'

'No. You just did.'

She glared at him, resenting the fact that he had tricked her more than the fact that he had found her out. 'Well, you needn't worry,' she informed him angrily. 'She didn't tell me anything. '

He leaned back in his seat and looked at her through lowered lids. 'I wasn't worried. Emma is one woman whose loyalty I have no doubts about. But it's funny, isn't it, how the guilty almost always give themselves away?'

Tanya didn't think it was funny at all.

He threw her a sarcastic smile. 'One of the drawbacks of having a conscience, you see.'

She glowered at her coffee-cup and refused to look at him. Maybe if she just ignored him he would go away. But he seemed to be in the mood for baiting her today.

'So much for your claim that you have no interest in my affairs. But then, I suppose one of the drawbacks of being a woman is your insatiable curiosity.' In one smooth movement he lowered the zipper of his tracksuit top, so that the front fell open to reveal his broad, sun-darkened chest. 'You can never bear just to leave well alone.'

'It strikes me that the biggest drawback any woman could have would be an association with you.' Instantly she rebuked herself. Why did she keep bringing their conversation on to a personal level? And, before he could trip her up again, she hurried on, 'What have you got against women, anyway?'

'Oh, I have nothing against women, believe me.' Amusement twinkled in his eyes. 'In spite of all their faults, I'm extremely partial to the fairer sex. In fact, I spend as much time as possible in their company.'

'No doubt.'

'But the trouble is I understand them far too well. They don't like that. Women like to believe that they're mysterious.'

'Maybe you spend time with the wrong sort of woman,' she replied as an image of the blonde in the restaurant flashed unsummoned across her mind. Then she added very pointedly, 'Of course, I suppose I shouldn't really judge. After all, I've observed only a very limited sample of the type of woman you prefer.'

She could see that he understood her perfectly. 'Fishing, Tanya?' he admonished—and she flushed at her own transparency. Then, 'What exactly is it that you wish to know?' he asked. 'My relationship with the lady I so rudely failed to introduce you to last night? Or just my sexual proclivities in a more general sense?'

'Neither.' She bit out the word, half wishing she'd had the sense just to drop the subject when she'd had the chance. But she couldn't resist adding, with a hint of almost prudish condemnation in her voice, 'She is your mistress, isn't she?'

A flash of something in his eyes: a mixture of amusement and surprise, she thought. 'That's a very old-fashioned word. What makes you think I have a mistress anyway?' he asked.

Lover, mistress, it was really all the same, though she slightly preferred the tag 'mistress' in this particular case. It seemed to suit the brash yet somehow furtive impression that the blonde countess had made. 'You probably have several,' she answered, staring with sudden intentness into his face. It seemed unlikely that Fausto Cabrini could be satisfied with one woman. His appetites in that direction, she guessed, would be as voracious as all his other appetites. In sex, he would be as tireless and demanding as he seemed to be in everything else. The notion provoked a warm sensation in her lower abdomen. Instantly she chased it away. 'Not that I'm really in the least bit interested, of course,' she said.

He laughed. 'You could have fooled me.' But he refrained from revealing whether the woman was his mistress or not, leaving her wondering, guessing, but somehow sure in the back of her mind that the answer was yes. 'To my ears,' he went on, 'you sounded like a typically curious representative of your sex. Why is it that women can never control their curiosity, especially with men? It seems to be in your genes. Somehow a woman can never resist the temptation to invite a man to bare his soul to her.'

'Don't flatter yourself. I can think of nothing more appalling than that you should bare your soul to me. Always supposing you have one, of course.'

He leaned towards her suddenly, taking her slightly by surprise, and folded his forearms on the table edge. The dark eyes observed her closely as he said, 'OK, I'll tell you what you want to know.'

Tell her what? About his mistresses, and all the other women in his life? She recoiled at the thought, was on the verge of protesting when he went on, 'The reason why my secretary left. I thought that was what all the fuss was about?'

'Of course.' What an idiot he must take her for.

'However, please keep what I'm about to tell you to yourself.' He leaned back in his chair again and folded his arms across his chest. 'When I told you that my secretary left of her own accord, that was absolutely true. Of course, if I'd known then what I know now, I'd have forced her to leave anyway. You see, this poor young innocent you're so concerned about was stealing from me, left, right and centre—and I might never have cottoned on if Emma hadn't caught her red-handed in my bedroom one day helping herself to a pair of my gold cuff-links.'

Tanya blinked at the figure in the blue tracksuit. She hadn't been expecting anything like this.

'She'd been working for me for about five years, and throughout that time, it transpired, she'd been lining her pockets pretty heavily.' A shadow crossed the lean, dark face, lending his features a harsh, almost satanic quality. 'They were small sums to start with, but they added up. Claims for expenses that were never used, a few thousand *lire* here and there from petty cash. If she'd stuck to that sort of thing, she would probably never have been found out. But, like all thieves, she became ambitious. Once when Renata was staying here a pair of her sapphire ear-rings disappeared. Renata assumed she had simply mislaid them and we thought no more about it. Then Emma reported that some of the silver from the kitchen had walked. She was worried that suspicion might fall on her.' His features softened for a moment as he smiled. 'Of course I know Emma and her family far too well to let such an idea even cross my mind.'

He sighed. 'Anyway, the pilfering continued. A little jade ornament here, a tie-pin there—until that fateful day when Emma caught her with the cuff-links. I was on business in Frankfurt at the time, but she wrote me a note, begging me not to go to the police, before packing her bags and catching the first train back to her family in Calabria.'

'Did you go to the police?'

'No, I didn't—for the same reason that I don't want the story spread around. When I got back, I did follow her down to Calabria, though, and forced her to return the few bits and pieces that she hadn't actually sold. She comes from a very poor family—and that, of course, was her excuse. They needed the money.' His mouth was set in a hard and unforgiving line as he went on, 'Hell, I can sympathise with poverty. I have a background not so many generations past, of the very direst poverty. But I can never have any sympathy with someone who steals. If she'd come to me and told me her family were in such desperate financial straits, I'd have given her the money she needed.'

'For a price, no doubt.' Tanya regretted the words almost before she had spoken them.

The expression in the dark eyes clouded. 'You're entitled to your opinion, of course.' The words came twisting contemptuously from his lips.

'I shouldn't have said that. I'm sorry.'

'As I said, you're entitled to your opinion.' He brushed her apology aside. 'I didn't go to the police, largely for her family's sake. And for the sake of her brother. She has a brother—an honest, hard-working boy—who runs his own small business in Varese, not far from here. It probably wouldn't have done his reputation much good if word had got around. But I put the fear of God into that sister of his. She'll never steal so much as a stalk of grass as long as she lives. Nor will she ever work in this part of Italy again.'

A cold shiver prickled down Tanya's spine. It didn't take much imagination to believe that part of his story anyway. Aroused to righteous anger, Fausto Cabrini would undoubtedly be a formidable and absolutely terrifying sight. It was a side of him that she had only glimpsed—and had no particular desire to see again.

A silence fell between them as he came to the end of his story. Then he added in a tone of pure malevolence, 'I don't like people who try to cheat me, you see.'

It was as though he had struck her a physical blow— and Tanya knew instinctively that he was retaliating against her own cruel remark. Perhaps she deserved it, but she winced all the same. 'My father didn't cheat you deliberately,' she defended bitterly, somehow knowing

in her heart that it was true, yet totally unable to explain
the reason why. 'I told you already he wouldn't do a
thing like that.'

'Except that that is exactly what he appears to have
done.'

'There must be some explanation. I'm absolutely sure
of it.'

'In that case, he will have the opportunity to enlighten
us personally on the matter in a week or so's time.'
Fausto Cabrini rose abruptly to his feet and glanced
down at her with a totally unreadable expression in his
eyes. 'When you and I will be taking a little trip to
Switzerland.'

The days went by with almost disconcerting speed.
They were long days and they were full—and Fausto
had not been joking when he'd told her how hard he
would make her work. In all honesty, Tanya had never
worked so hard in all her life. But the work, to her
amazement, was enjoyable, and she was soon taking
secret pride in the fact that she managed to keep up with
the demanding pace that Fausto set.

He taught her the basics of how to use the computer
and proved himself a patient and perceptive teacher—as
well as the sort of boss who knew exactly when and how
to delegate. By the time the three months were up,
Tanya felt certain, she would know how to run a
business standing on her head.

Frequently Fausto worked over lunch or late into the
night, and then Tanya took the opportunity to get out
the sketch-pad she had driven into the local village one
afternoon to buy, and do some work on her designs for
the old wash-house. Bearing in mind the story that
Fausto had told her about his great-great-grandmother
who had once worked as a washerwoman on the estate,
she had decided on a distinctly olde worlde approach.

Chintz and chenille for the draperies, simple, rustic-looking furniture, and maybe a couple of tapestries on the walls. The sort of ambience, in fact, in which the old lady herself might possibly have felt at home.

As she secretly beavered away on her designs, her enthusiasm for the project grew. Her ideas, she knew, might possibly fail to coincide with what Fausto had in mind, but that was a risk she would have to take. She hadn't even mentioned to him that she had started on the job—and he had never raised the subject again. When she presented him with her preliminary sketches, she thought to herself with a smug little smile, he would be totally taken by surprise.

For the trip to Switzerland she had picked out one of the few stylish dresses she had brought with her, one of her favourites, in crisp white lawn which she wore with a broad tan leather belt and matching tan and white sandals. That morning, she brushed her shoulder-length gold hair into a shining billow of curls and applied a minimum of make-up. With the light tan she had acquired over the past few days it was all she needed. Then, after a quick breakfast—just a cup of Emma's deliciously frothy capuccino and a slice of toast—she hurried outside, anxious to get started with the day. A portentous day, she felt instinctively, one that was destined to leave its mark.

Fausto was waiting for her out in the forecourt by the car, dressed in a cool white jacket that emphasised his muscular shape, light grey trousers encasing the long, athletic legs. The soft white shirt was open at the neck, revealing the strong, tanned column of his throat. He smiled at her. '*Buon giorno.* You're looking very beautiful today.' The dark eyes travelled over her quite openly, taking in the tiny waist, lingering over the full, voluptuous swell of her breasts, admiring the slim lines of her shapely legs.

To her annoyance, the compliment brought a faint blush to Tanya's cheeks, but she managed to sweep past him with a show of indifference as he held the door of the Lamborghini open for her.

'Good morning,' she replied. Then she settled herself with composure in the low-slung bucket seat, adjusting the skirt of her dress over her knees.

He slid into the driver's seat beside her and glanced at his watch. 'We should be in Lugano by nine o'clock. It's just about an hour's drive.'

She nodded, knowing what was coming next. They had already been over all this a dozen times the night before.

'I'll drop you off at the clinic, then go back into town myself. I have some business there. You talk to your father and tell him I know about the icon.' The dark eyes glanced across at her. 'When I get back to pick you up I shall expect a full and convincing explanation. Tell him that. I shall try to get back to the clinic before twelve o'clock. That should give him ample time to think something up.'

Tanya flashed him an irritated look. 'He won't have any need to think something up. I'm sure all he has to do is tell the truth.' Then her eyes narrowed in cautious reproof. 'He's a sick man, remember. Try not to be too hard on him.'

'Rest assured that I shall treat him as he deserves.' He gave her a look that warned that wheedling would be a waste of time. He wouldn't even listen if she tried that.

Tanya said nothing, but crossed her fingers mentally. If her father had ever needed to talk his way out of a corner in the past, he certainly needed to talk his way out of a pretty tight one now. The man at her side was still capable of breaking him financially. And financial ruin at this stage, she knew, would break him totally.

For the most part, the road to Lugano was a winding,

country road, twisting and turning its way through breathtaking scenery as it carried them up to Bellinzona and the border and through the foothills of the Alps. But Tanya's mind was not on the scenery as she watched the kilometres flash by. The figure at her side seemed blissfully unaware of it as he negotiated the dips and bends of the road with his customary faultless skill—if at somewhat less than his customary speed—but Tanya was dreading this meeting with her father more than she had ever dreaded anything.

At just before nine, they were skimming round the outskirts of Lugano, heading the few kilometres east to where her father's clinic was situated. And what seemed like only moments later, the Lamborghini gritted to a halt on the gravel driveway outside the main door. 'I'll see you some time before twelve,' Fausto told her, his eyes expressionless as she climbed out. Then, with a deep, throaty growl, the big car moved away.

A trim receptionist with a neat chignon greeted Tanya as she walked nervously into the airy, sunlit entrance hall. 'Miss Sinclair, how lovely to see you! Your father is expecting you. He's out in the garden. If you would just like to follow me?'

The Heinrich Castelli Clinic had more the luxurious air of a five-star hotel than of an institution designed to care for the sick, Tanya reflected wryly as she followed the brisk, efficient figure down deeply carpeted corridors lined with velvet-upholstered sofas and potted plants. Fausto Cabrini had obviously been feeling generous when he picked this place.

They were approaching a wide, glass-fronted veranda that led to the garden and Tanya felt the knot of apprehension tighten in her breast. It was almost four weeks since she had last seen her father, and though she had spoken briefly to him on the telephone he had no idea of the upheaval that had occurred in his daughter's life since he had left for Switzerland, and even less idea of the cause of it.

Just before they stepped outside, she touched the receptionist diffidently on the arm. 'How is my father? Is he well?'

The woman responded with a warm, compassionate nod of her well groomed head. 'He's just fine, Miss Sinclair. Improving a little every day. Come,' she added with a reassuring smile, 'see for yourself.'

Devlin saw her before she saw him. By the time she was half-way across the grass to the garden seat where he had been sitting leafing idly through a copy of the *Herald Tribune*, he was on his feet and waving to her. 'Tanya, darling!'

She ran the last few yards and threw herself with sudden delight into his arms. Oh, it was wonderful to see him! And he *was* looking well, she noted with relief. In neat dark slacks and short-sleeved cotton shirt, he had acquired a healthy bit of colour and the blue eyes seemed less sunken, more alive. Tanya kissed him warmly on the cheek and pulled him down beside her on the garden seat. 'Father, you look terrific!'

Even his smile was brighter than it had been for a long, long time. 'I feel terrific, Tanya. Like a new man. And, if I may say so, you're looking pretty terrific yourself. Life at the Villa Cabrini obviously agrees with you.'

She smiled a light, ambiguous smile. 'I'm being kept busy.' And she hugged his arm. 'At a guess, I'd even say you've put on a pound or two.'

'I have. Two and a half kilos, to be precise. And no wonder. The food they serve you here would tempt a supplicant!' He laughed, and the very sound of that laughter warmed the depths of Tanya's heart. It seemed like years since she had heard him laugh like that. 'Good food, good wine, good sunshine and really excellent medical care.' He winked at her, but there was an unmistakable note of seriousness as he went on, 'You can stop worrying about me, Tanya. I've a bit to go before I'm back to full strength yet, but I'm getting there. I'll be on my feet again before the summer's out, I promise you.'

Looking at him, it wasn't too difficult to believe. A month ago he had seemed like a man on the brink of death; now he was clearly on the mend. And as he regaled her cheerfully with details of the last few weeks, she was only too happy to postpone the evil moment when she would have to shatter his almost carefree mood by bringing up the subject of the fake icon. There was no saying what that—and the inevitable confrontation with Fausto Cabrini—would do to him.

It was later, as they enjoyed coffee and biscuits in the clinic's exquisitely coverted orangery, that Tanya finally forced herself to take the plunge. And, ironically, the opportunity presented itself when Devlin began singing Fausto Cabrini's praises to her.

'I was so glad when I heard you'd gone to work for him,' he told her, helping himself to his second *langue de chat*. 'Much more agreeable than a summer in Vienna, I'm sure. Dull place, Vienna.' Then he went on, on an earnest note, 'I owe that young man my life, you know. The doctors may have saved me from dying, but it was Fausto Cabrini who gave me back my will to live.'

Tanya took a deep breath and reached out a hand to touch her father's arm. 'He knows about the icon, Father. He knows that it's a fake.'

For a long, uncomfortable moment Devlin didn't speak. Then, very carefully, he brushed a couple of stray crumbs from his lips. 'I knew he was bound to find out eventually,' he said, 'but I would have preferred to tell him myself.'

So it was true. 'Why, Father?' Tanya looked

helplessly into the pale blue eyes.

He avoided her question and countered anxiously with one of his own. 'Was he very angry?' he wanted to know.

Tanya smiled a bitter smile, remembering the fury in Cabrini's face that evening he had burst in on her at home and demanded her immediate presence in Italy. But there was no need for Devlin to know that. She nodded. 'He was angry. But why did you do it, Father? Why did you give him the icon when you knew it was a fake? And why for all these years did you pretend to me that it was valuable?' A dull mix of hurt and confusion quivered in her voice.

Her father looked across at her with an expression of heartfelt regret. 'Tanya, please try to understand. When I gave that icon to Fausto Cabrini, deceiving him was the last thing on my mind. I've just told you I know I owe that man my life. When I invited him to choose some work of art as a kind of surety I never thought for one moment that he'd choose that. And when he did, if you remember, I tried to talk him out of it.'

The blue eyes held the tawny ones, urgently begging to be believed. 'But I couldn't bring myself to tell him then that it was a fake. Not because I wanted to deceive him—but because I desperately didn't want to disappoint you.' He sighed. 'You see, I've always known it was a fake. The original eighteenth-century piece that your Grandpa Boris smuggled out of Russia all those years ago was evidently lost or stolen along the way—and replaced by the late nineteenth-century copy that he gave to Natasha and me on our wedding day. Your mother never knew it was a fake. She loved that little icon—as I do, and you do, too, I know—and I wanted her to go on believing it was the original.' His voice broke as he added quietly, 'I wanted you to go on believing it, too. I'm sorry the truth had to come out this way.'

Tanya clasped her father's bony hand in hers. 'I understand,' she said. 'But, really, you didn't have to pretend to me.'

He shifted his eyes upward to look at her again. 'What time did you say Signor Cabrini was coming?' he asked.

She squeezed his hand. 'Some time before twelve.' She glanced down quickly at her watch. 'It's after eleven-thirty now. He could be here at any time.'

Devlin started to rise determinedly to his feet. 'Let's wait for him in the entrance hall,' he said, taking his daughter's arm. 'I don't want him to think I'm hiding in the shadows like a thief.'

Tanya said nothing as they slowly started to traverse the thickly carpeted corridor that led back to the entrance hall. Her thoughts were a jumble, too complicated even to begin to sort out now. And, though her father's story had touched her—and in her eyes largely exonerated him of guilt—she found herself unable to judge what the reaction of the central figure in this little drama was going to be. And, as she was all too painfully aware, it was his reaction that mattered most.

Her thoughts trailed off abruptly as a tall, dark figure, broad-shouldered in a crisp white linen jacket, light grey trousers and soft white shirt appeared unexpectedly at the end of the corridor, moving in strong, brisk strides towards them. And an unidentifiable emotion hit Tanya at the sight of him: part apprehension, resentment and anxiety—but with an undeniable twist of pleasure mingled in. He looked so inordinately handsome, she thought, and it was the first time she had openly acknowledged that to herself. In sudden confusion, she lowered her eyes.

Devlin was the first to speak, deliberately straightening his spine as he addressed his words to the younger man. 'I owe you a few explanations,' he said. 'Let's find a quiet corner and sit down.'

The little group moved to the far end of the entrance hall where a cluster of armchairs was arranged, and sat down facing one another with an air of polite solemnity. Cabrini leaned back in his chair and nodded to Devlin, an indication that he should begin. Tanya held her breath and prayed. Please let him be feeling merciful today.

He listened without saying a word, the dark eyes averted, his lips set in a firm, straight line. The long-fingered hands were laid lightly along the arms of his chair, one leg balanced casually at the ankle across one muscular, grey-clad thigh. It was not a belligerent pose, Tanya tried to reassure herself, though neither was it a particularly compassionate one. Detached and contemplative seemed to be the best description of his current frame of mind—and she had learned over the past two weeks that, from here, his mood could quite easily swing either way.

And she watched anxiously for that subtle tightening in his lower jaw, the impatient flexing of his strong brown hands or the faintest narrowing of the long-lashed lids that would inevitably presage a storm. But as Devlin came to the end of his tale, Cabrini leaned forward slightly in his seat and ran an open palm across his thick black hair—and Tanya felt the knot of tension in her slacken imperceptibly. There seemed to be some hope that her prayers might be answered after all.

'So you see,' Devlin was anxiously assuring him, 'the only reason I withheld the truth was for my daughter's sake. I had no intention whatsoever of deceiving you. I hope you will forgive a foolish and romantic old man.'

'I see.' Cabrini gazed down at the space between the two men as he spoke. 'Of course, it would have been preferable if you had told me right away. You will understand that it came as something of a shock to discover that the pledge I had been given was a fake. And a most unpleasant shock at that.' The dark eyes lifted to scrutinise the worn face of the older man. 'I am not a man who takes kindly to being deceived.' He sat back in his seat and drew in a long and ominous breath—and Tanya felt her knuckles clench, remembering the unforgiving story he had told about his former secretary. Then he let out his breath on a short, almost impatient sigh. 'In the circumstances, however, I am prepared to overlook this small discourtesy. We shall say no more about it. The matter is closed.'

Relief showed plainly on Devlin's face. 'Of course, I shall arrange for the remaining few paintings that I have to be shipped to you immediately. I hope you will accept them as a replacement token of my pledge.'

'That will not be necessary. I shall keep the icon as we originally agreed—and hope to return it to you in due course.' And his eyes flicked momentarily in Tanya's direction as he added with a meaningful smile, 'I think I already have all the guarantees I need.'

Devlin nodded. 'Believe me, there is nothing in the world I would work harder to redeem. That little icon means more to me than any other possession that I own.'

Fausto Cabrini rose abruptly to his feet. 'We have to go now, I'm afraid.' He nodded to Tanya. 'Ready?'

She embraced her father, sharing his relief, and kissed him warmly on the cheek. 'Take care, Father. I'll try to come back and see you again soon.'

Devlin eased himself from his chair and, in an almost formal gesture, offered Cabrini his hand. 'Thank you,' he said simply Then he added with a paternal smile, 'Please look after her for me.'

A moment later, Tanya and Fausto were heading quickly across the entrance hall, through the door and down the steps to the waiting car. Tanya could scarcely believe that it had all been sorted out so amicably, and she felt a warm surge of gratitude towards the tall, dark figure who pulled open the door of the Lamborghini and stood aside to let her climb inside. In a totally automatic response, she paused for the barest of seconds and threw him a genuinely appreciative smile.

The dark eyes locked with hers. 'Don't think you're wriggling out of anything,' he said. 'Our deal still stands. Besides,' as he climbed in next to her and slammed the door shut, 'you heard what your father said. He wants me to look after you.'

Tanya took instant exception to the amused note in his voice. 'That really won't be necessary,' she snapped. 'I don't need anyone to look after me. Least of all you.'

But Fausto merely smiled an enigmatic smile as he thrust the key into the ignition and the engine of the big car throbbed to instant life. 'We shall see, Tanya,' he murmured, almost to himself. 'We shall see.'

CHAPTER SIX

'WHY did you do it?' Tanya asked.

They had stopped for lunch at a trattoria on the banks of Lake Lugano, just a few kilometres outside the city. The day had grown warm and the tables were thronged with hungry, thirsty holiday-makers taking a break from the round of sailing, sunbathing and sightseeing. At a nod from Fausto, the waiter had found them a quiet corner in the little covered courtyard outside and left them to study the menu. He glanced at her over the top of it now. 'Why did I do what?' he asked, though Tanya could read in the dark eyes that he understood perfectly what she had meant.

'Why were you so lenient with my father? I thought you'd want to teach him a lesson, at least.'

His eyes held hers across the red-checked tablecloth. 'Did I disappoint you, Tanya? I must apologise.'

She grimaced. 'On the contrary. But I am surprised. I didn't think you'd fall for such a sentimental little tale— the doting father who risks his honour to protect the foolish fantasies of his spoilt daughter. The whole romantic story that surrounds the little icon, as a matter of fact. To tell the truth, I wouldn't have been in the least surprised if you'd just laughed the whole thing out of court.' She paused and threw him a subtly challenging smile. 'But I was wrong. Perhaps, after all, you have a heart.'

He leaned back a little in his chair and casually hooked one white-clad arm over its slatted wooden back. 'Has it ever occurred to you, Tanya,' he said, 'that the money I lent your father is little more than a drop in the ocean to me? I won't miss it, even if he never pays me back. And

107

as for the icon—I could buy myself a dozen of the genuine article any day of the week. The fact that the one your father gave me is worthless is a matter of no importance when it comes down to it.'

Tanya couldn't resist a teasing smile. 'You don't have to be so defensive,' she said. 'Why don't you just admit that his sad little story struck some chord with you?'

Fausto tossed aside his menu and turned to snap his fingers at the waiter who came scurrying across. 'We'll order now.' The shrewd, dark eyes in the strong, tanned face were inscrutable as he glanced across at her. 'I suggest the *spaghetti carbonara* followed by fresh trout. Is that OK with you?'

A deliberate evasion. She nodded. 'That's fine.'

'And bring us a bottle of your best Frascati. That will be all.'

As the waiter moved away, she leaned her elbows on the table and stared intently across at him. 'You haven't answered my question,' she said.

An amused smile played around the corners of his lips. 'Why do I get the impression that you're trying to lay bare my soul again? I thought I'd already made it clear to you that it's a waste of time.'

'Of course. I forgot—no soul, no conscience, and now, you'd like me to believe, no heart. You really are a hard man, aren't you?' Her tone was light-hearted, bantering.

'Maybe.' He paused as a sudden graveness filled his eyes, and he watched her, as though wondering whether she would fully understand what he was going on to say. 'You see, I've seen what too much conscience, soul and heart can do. It can destroy a person. I've watched it happen. It's a frightening thing.'

'You're talking about your mother, aren't you?' She had no idea how she had known that, but she did.

He nodded, glancing down at the tablecloth. 'My mother was a woman who allowed herself to be eaten alive by her own virtues. Or weaknesses, if you prefer to call them that. Married to a different type of man, it might have been different for her. But my father abused her goodness—her devotion, her trust. He simply trampled all over them. And she let him. That was the saddest thing.' He shook his head. 'My mother died a long, long time before they buried her.'

A silence fell, then he raised his eyes at last to look at her again. 'So you see why I decided a long time ago that those were three attributes I'd be better off without?'

She wanted to reach out and touch him, but she did not dare. 'I think you're wrong to think like that,' she said. 'It doesn't always have to be that way.'

'No?' Cynicism tugged at his lip. 'Well, let's just say I have no plans to give history the chance to repeat itself.'

She smiled. 'So you're a man in charge of your own destiny?' An effort to tease him from his sudden gloomy mood. 'That must be very reassuring to know.'

He gave her a long look and some message seemed to pass between the two of them that neither was capable, at that moment, of deciphering. It spoke of understanding, trust. He said, 'I'm not the only one who's been giving secrets away today.'

Tanya looked at him in puzzlement.

'Your sketches for the wash-house. I had a look at them.'

Abruptly Tanya's expression grew serious. She had finished the sketches late last night and slipped them under his office door, uncertain whether he was still there or not. Now she waited to find out what he thought of them with a sudden, anxious tightening in her throat.

He touched the tips of his long, tanned fingers together and regarded her over the apex of his hands. 'As I said, they're very revealing—and very good.'

'Do you really like them?' It was suddenly important to her that he should.

'I like them very much. I think they're excellent.'

Then he smiled. 'No need to blush. There are just a couple of points I'd like to make. Perhaps we can go over them together this evening after dinner.'

Tanya couldn't suppress a grin. 'I was a little bit worried that you might be expecting something more modern.'

'Not at all. You've done them exactly as I wanted them.' His lips pursed thoughtfully as he stared across at the pleased, flushed face with its halo of bright gold curls. And his eyes seemed to linger and admire the smooth skin of her neck and shoulders, lightly tanned against the soft white of her dress. 'You're really full of surprises, aren't you?' he added unexpectedly.

It was probably just as well that the waiter chose that moment to arrive with their two plates of spaghetti and bottle of chilled wine. The compliment, so simply and spontaneously spoken, had taken Tanya by surprise. And she sensed that Fausto slightly regretted it. He glanced down quickly at his watch as the waiter moved away again. 'I forgot to mention it,' he said, 'but we have an appointment in Novara at three o'clock.'

They were on the road again in just over an hour, heading back to the Italian border. Tanya was feeling thoroughly pleased with the way the day had gone so far. The messy little business about the icon had been neatly resolved and her father's honour salvaged, if not totally restored. And, equally pleasing, her designs for the wash-house had been approved—and not just approved, praised pretty lavishly! She had every reason to feel satisfied.

Yet, underlying the sense of well-being that the day's progress had brought to her was an unmistakable undercurrent of uneasiness. It had started, she sensed, at that moment when Fausto had so unexpectedly material-ised at the end of the clinic corridor—and had peaked with their strangely intimate conversation over lunch. It was an odd sort of uneasiness, bordering on excitement, as though the powerful and disturbing feelings that his presence seemed automatically to arouse in her had somehow grown to be almost pleasurable. And that was alarming in itself. Hadn't she already warned herself that she must be totally immune to him? She would simply have to try a little harder, that was all.

When they reached the old town of Novara, nestling amid the rocky green hills of Piedmont, some fifty kilometres west of Milan, it was just before three. The big white car drew to a silent halt outside one of the fine old *palazzos* in the quiet, siesta-stilled city centre, and Fausto leaned across her to open the passenger door. 'This is where my client lives,' he informed her. 'Our business shouldn't take too long.'

Involuntarily, Tanya stiffened as his arm brushed momentarily against her breast, and she felt herself flush at the faint smile her reaction brought to his lips. Then she took a deep breath to compose herself as she stepped out quickly on to the cobbled street, walked behind Fausto to the huge, carved wooden door and waited as he rang the bell. A woman's voice answered almost immediately on the entry-phone. Briefly Fausto announced himself and a second later the door buzzed open to let them in.

The interior of the building seemed cool and dark after the bright sunshine. A lift bore them swiftly and silently to the third floor, then the doors swished open to release them again.

'Fausto *caro*!' A blonde-haired woman in skin-fitting leather trousers and a brightly coloured loose silk shirt was waiting for them. Tanya gaped in stunned silence as she threw herself into Fausto's arms. She had recognised her instantly, of course. It was the countess; the woman she had seen that evening in the restaurant.

Tanya watched with a thinly tolerant smile as kisses were exchanged, and noted that the woman seemed reluctant to let Fausto go. But she slid away from him at last and turned to her second guest with what, had it not been for the glint of cold steel in her eyes, would have passed for a ravishingly dazzling smile. 'And who is this delightful young person you've brought along with you?' One red-tipped hand was still clasped firmly round Fausto's arm as she spoke.

Tanya glared into the brightly made-up, dark green eyes. The woman had recognised her too, of course, but had evidently decided to feign otherwise. Silly woman, she decided. What was she worried about?

As Fausto made the introductions Tanya sensed that he was perfectly aware of the raw hostility that suddenly sizzled in the air, and perhaps even enjoying it. 'I'd like you to meet my new assistant, Miss Tanya Sinclair. Tanya, my dear friend the Contessa Beatrice Alberto Lombardi Riccangeli. Or Bea for short.'

The countess laughed delightedly, parting perfectly painted, bright red lips to reveal a set of small, white, even teeth. 'Definitely Bea for short. Who could possibly remember that enormous mouthful of silly names?' Her English was perfect. With a clank of gold chains, she offered her free hand for Tanya to shake.

Tanya took it stiffly. 'How do you do?'

They were led into a vividly furnished room, rich with heavy velvet furnishings and sparkling crystal chandeliers. Fausto sat down in what Tanya suspected with a flash of annoyance was his customary chair, long legs stretched out casually in front of him, evidently very much at home. Tanya deposited herself on a chaise-longue by the window, while the countess curled up, catlike, on a nearby divan. She smoothed the supple leather of her trousers over her slender thighs and contemplated her long, red fingernails as she smiled, 'You're English, aren't you? What part of England are you from?'

'Sussex.' So it was questions-and-answers time.

'I do love England. And the English. Don't you, Fausto?' the countess enquired over her shoulder. 'Such polite, well mannered people, I find.'

The dark eyes drifted across to Tanya with a provocative smile. 'Some of them,' he consented lightly. 'Some of the time.'

Tanya threw him a stiff smile in response as the countess went on, 'My late husband, the count, was distantly related to the Skinners of Sussex. A very old family. You must know them?' One carefully pencilled eyebrow lifted questioningly.

Tanya shook her head. 'No, I'm afraid not.' So the woman was a widow. And that little revelation somehow irked her all the more. She would have been happier to learn the countess had a husband tucked away somewhere.

'And is this your first visit to Italy?'

'Not exactly—though it is my first experience of working here.'

'That must be very interesting for you.'

Tanya nodded and pinned a tight smile on her face, waiting for the next question. She was saved from further interrogation, however, by the appearance of a uniformed maid balancing a vast silver tray of tea and cakes. These were distributed with considerable ceremony, as well as several shy smiles cast in Fausto's direction—confirming Tanya's earlier suspicion that he was a regular visitor at the house. In spite of her recent and fairly substantial lunch, she helped herself to a generous slice of fluffy-looking chocolate cake. At least, if she was eating, she couldn't be expected to answer any more questions for a while.

But she needn't have worried as it turned out. The countess had evidently tired for the time being of her little questions-and-answers game and had removed herself from the divan and produced a sheaf of papers from a bureau drawer. Then, with a cursory, 'Excuse us, my dear. Business calls,' tossed casually in Tanya's direction, she installed her slim figure somewhat precariously on the arm of Fausto's chair.

Tanya sipped absent-mindedly at the fine Darjeeling brew in the delicate pale green Limoges cup and observed the scene in front of her from lowered lids. If this is strictly a business meeting, she told herself, then I'm a monkey's maiden aunt. The bright blonde tresses were virtually resting against Fausto's head, the shiny red lips barely a fraction from his handsome nose as the pair of them bent over the clearly compelling contents of the documents. Perhaps the woman needs glasses, she found herself surmising on a sour note, abandoning midway her slice of chocolate cake. Suddenly she didn't feel like eating any more.

At length the cosy little conference was adjourned.

'Tanya, my dear, so sorry we've been neglecting you.' The countess slid, catlike, from her perch on Fausto's chair—why did she keep comparing the wretched woman to a cat? Tanya wondered drily to herself—and dropped to her leather-clad knees beside his feet, one slender arm slung casually across his grey-clad thigh. She made a small face and flexed her head delicately to one side. 'Darling, I've got a crick in my neck,' she told him in a breathless voice.

'We can't have that.' The long, tanned fingers curved to her nape in a gentle, lingering massage—and was it Tanya's imagination, or did the dark eyes momentarily seek her own before elaborating, 'It's such a very pretty neck.'

The countess sighed and glanced slyly at Tanya. 'He's so clever with his hands.'

I'll bet. But she didn't say the words out loud. Instead she just glared down at her empty teacup and began to wish that she had waited outside.

The countess straightened with a little moan as Fausto leaned back once more in his chair. 'Much better now,' she purred and fixed Tanya with her cold green eyes.

'You've been so quiet, dear. Why don't you tell me all about yourself?'

Tanya could have listed without too much difficulty at least a score of reasons why, but none that was adequately civil sprang immediately to mind. 'There's not much to tell,' she answered airily. 'I'm just an old friend of the family come to help Fausto out in the office for a while.' She glared across at him, wishing she could think of some way to dislodge the smug smile from his face. 'Isn't that right?'

'Oh, Tanya's being much too modest,' he declared. 'She's a girl of many talents, as I'm discovering all the time. She's doing a lot more than just helping me out in the office. Why don't you tell Bea about the little decorating job you're doing for me?'

The cat's eyes widened with sudden interest. 'How exciting! Do tell.'

Tanya shrugged. 'It's just a simple decorating job.' She was not being modest. The truth was she was totally mesmerised by the feline hand now moving down to rest quite openly on Fausto's knee. The hand began a slow and tentative caress.

Then Fausto spoke. 'It's the old wash-house. Tanya's going to do it up for me. And from what I've seen of the sketches she's done, she's going to do a pretty stunning job.' He paused and glanced across at Tanya as though expecting some reaction to his words of praise. But she only stared back at him with hostile, narrowed eyes. What was he waiting for to remove that ridiculous woman's paw from his knee? Was he actually enjoying it so much that he had lost all sense of propriety?

'But that's splendid!' The red lips curved in a plastic smile. 'Haven't I been telling you for years, Fausto dear, that that little place could be turned into an absolute gem? With the right decorators, of course.' She addressed herself to Tanya with a hint of acid in her voice. 'I suppose you've done this sort of thing before?'

Tanya felt the muscles in her jaw tighten. 'I don't take on jobs I'm not qualified to do, if that's what you're implying,' she shot back, almost forgetting in her indignation that this particular job had been forced on her. Who did the abominable woman think she was?

Fausto shifted in his chair, an amused smile flitting across his face as he turned to look across at her. Damn you! Tanya thought, meeting his gaze with an uncompromising flash of anger in her eyes. You're actually enjoying this pathetic little sparring match! It appeals to your superior male conceit to have two females squabbling in front of you!

'Bea may be able to help you,' he offered now, an edge of incitement in his voice. 'She has contacts in the design business. Furniture, furnishings—that kind of thing.' He patted the countess's slim, brown arm. 'I'm sure you'd be glad to offer Tanya any help she needs?'

'Of course. I'd be only too happy to oblige.' This was accompanied by another calculatedly dazzling smile.

'That's very kind of you, I'm sure.' A weak smile here—but she could hardly turn the offer down.

The countess was on to a winning streak. 'Will it be ready in time for the party, do you think?'

What party? Tanya's blank look clearly revealed she hadn't a clue what the woman was talking about.

'But hasn't Fausto told you?' There was a note of triumph in the purring voice. 'Why, my dear, your employer's renowned for his annual summer party. It's the highspot of the season. People simply flock from far and wide. You *must* have your little decorating job finished by then. We'll all be dying to see it.' She swivelled round and perched her chin coquettishly on Fausto's knee. 'You're not going to disappoint us, *caro*, I hope. Summer wouldn't be summer without the grand Cabrini ball.'

Fausto smiled down at her indulgently. 'You know I wouldn't dream of disappointing you,' he said. Then he glanced at the thin gold watch at his wrist. 'Time for us to go, I'm afraid.' And, disentangling himself from the countess's embrace—though, Tanya noted, not with any particular haste—he rose to his feet and added, 'I have to get back for a call from the States.'

'What a busy man you are.' The countess scrambled to his side, slipping one arm possessively through his as she followed him reluctantly out to the hall. 'Always rushing off somewhere.'

He bent to kiss her on both cheeks. '*Ciao*, Bea. I'll see you soon.'

The two women exchanged a cool handshake. 'A pleasure to meet you.'

'Likewise.'

'And don't let that boss of yours forget about the party,' came the shrill reminder as the lift doors closed. 'I'll never forgive him if he does.'

Tanya was still bristling when they got outside. She barely even glanced at Fausto as he held open the door of the car for her and she climbed inside. The day had appeared to be going so well up until a couple of hours ago. What a ridiculous encounter! What an absolutely idiotic waste of time!

He slid his long frame easily into the low seat at her side. 'I'm sorry if Bea ruffled your feathers,' he observed with casual insincerity, gunning the engine and slipping smoothly into gear.

Tanya kept her eyes fixed unflinchingly ahead. 'She didn't ruffle my feathers,' she retorted tartly. 'She just doesn't happen to be my type of person, that's all.'

The big car moved silently away from the pavement edge. 'Oh, and what type of person would you say she was?' Subtle amusement was taunting in his voice.

'Your type of person, I would guess.' A hint of malice now in hers.

He laughed out loud, a rich, deep laugh that somehow only irritated Tanya more. 'Is that a compliment or an insult, Tanya dear?'

The spurious endearment made her grit her teeth. 'Neither. A mere statement of fact. I would say she was your type of person to a tee—shallow, supercilious and showy.'

She half expected him to be annoyed, but he only laughed again, then turned with a smile to look at her. 'My, my,' he observed silkily, 'you're showing your claws.'

Tanya sniffed derisively, her eyes still riveted firmly on the road ahead. 'I can't stand fawning females,' she informed him cuttingly. 'Though I'm not surprised that, like most men, you're not impartial to them yourself.'

'As I've already told you, I'm partial to all sorts of women. And luckily there seems to be a huge variety of sorts available.'

'And none more available than the countess, no doubt.'

He turned to look at her again and, almost in spite of herself, Tanya swivelled round to meet his eyes. 'Why, Tanya, I do believe you're jealous,' he accused her with a quiet smile.

'How utterly ridiculous!' She swung away from him, face flaming. Well, it *was* ridiculous, wasn't it? How could she possibly be jealous of him? She stared hard at the road again as they left the city limits behind and the big car gradually began to gather speed. It was simply that intolerable woman who had made her mad, irked her beyond reason with her pathetic feline overtures.

Again in her mind's eye she saw the languorous arm draped oh-so-casually across Fausto's thigh, the blonde coquettish head virtually nestling against his, the small hand gently caressing his knee with an almost insolent familiarity. And again she felt the dull ache of anger that had assailed her then, only fiercer and more threatening now as she finally acknowledged it for what it really was

Not anger at all, but raw, undiluted jealousy.

No! As abruptly as the truth had dawned, she swept it frantically away. She'd been crazy even to allow the thought to cross her mind. He stirred her physically, admittedly—to a degree that both disturbed and frightened her—but that was something she could handle, simply by ignoring it. And there really was no more to it than that. The Countess Bea, along with all the other women in his life, was more than welcome to him. Fausto Cabrini didn't mean a thing to her.

All the way back to the villa she repeated this conviction over and over again to herself, like a child struggling to commit to memory some particularly difficult piece of poetry. By the time they swept up the driveway to the big front door, she had practically convinced herself that it was true.

Fausto disappeared straight away into his office, leaving Tanya to spend what remained of the afternoon as she pleased. It was something of a relief when Emma came to tell her she would be dining alone. The *signor*, the plump-faced woman informed her pleasantly, was still tied up with work. He would see her later for a drink in the library.

So she had a couple more hours to collect herself, to drive all the silly, unsettling notions from her head. She showered and changed into a simple cotton skirt and matching top. By the time he summoned her to join him in the library—for 'summon' her was exactly what he would do, knowing him—she would be calm and relaxed and totally in command of her senses again. She would prove to him, without even having to bring the subject up, that this afternoon he had misunderstood her totally. Neither jealousy nor any other such emotion entered into her feelings for him.

After a solitary dinner, during which, in spite of her resolution, Tanya was unable to whip up much of an appetite, she went back to her room and made a fruitless attempt to read a book. About ten o'clock the blue phone rang.

'I'm in the library,' was all he said. 'Come down and join me for a drink.'

Her summons.

She did her best to walk sedately down the stairs, though her heart was racing, and she fought hard to ignore the clench of excitement in the pit of her stomach as, with a foolishly trembling hand, she pushed open the library door. Why was her body such a traitor to her mind? Why was it refusing to obey the messages that she was sending from her brain?

'Come on in. I've already fixed your drink for you.' He was seated in one of the deep-cushioned armchairs, two tall glasses set on the low, brass coffee-table in front of him. 'Sit down.' He indicated the armchair next to his own. 'I'm sorry I couldn't join you for dinner. There were a couple of things that needed tying up.'

She smiled a bright smile. 'So Emma said. Did you manage to get it all done?'

'Just about.' He seemed unaware of the tension in her, himself apparently totally at ease. He had changed since she had seen him earlier and was wearing a short-sleeved, blue-striped shirt and a pair of faded denim jeans. The strongly muscled arms were deeply bronzed and shadowed with fine, dark hairs from elbow to wrist. Funny, she pondered, something quickening disloyally inside her at the thought, but she hadn't really noticed that before. The powerful column of his throat arched back as he leaned against the cushion at his head and gazed across at her through lowered lids.

'I have good news for you,' he said, a faint smile curling at the corners of his lips. 'I'm leaving for New York tomorrow. I'll be away for about ten days.'

'That's nice.' It was a reflex response. A reflex from her brain, but not her heart.

'Yes, I thought you'd be pleased.' He leaned across and pushed the glass of martini closer to her, then raised his own glass slowly to his lips. 'You'll be in charge of the office while I'm gone. I'm sure you'll cope.'

She smiled a tight smile, wishing she felt as overjoyed as she ought to at his unexpected piece of news. It was exactly what she had been wanting, after all. Room to manoeuvre. A chance to rebuild the defences she had so foolishly let fall. But she felt no joy. Only a sudden, uneasy tightening somewhere in the region of her heart.

He reached down for the folder that was lying at his feet. 'I've got your sketches here—but I don't really think there's any need for us to go through them in detail. They're fine.' The dark eyes scrutinised her face. 'In fact, as I told you earlier, they're more than just fine, they're excellent. I've made one or two comments— suggestions more than anything else. You'll see for yourself.' He laid the folder on the table between them. 'I'd no idea you'd been doing all this work outside office hours.'

She shrugged, taking a mouthful of her drink and tasting nothing. 'You said you wanted me to get on with it. Besides, it's what I enjoy doing. Once I got started, I found it difficult to lay it aside.'

He sat back and regarded her with interest in his eyes. His hair seemed very dark against the cushion at his head. 'I really misjudged you, didn't I?'

'What do you mean?' Something in the way he was looking at her was raising goosebumps on her flesh.

'In the beginning. Don't tell me you've forgotten already all the dreadful things I said?'

If only he would say them all again so she could hate him like she used to do! She shrugged again. 'Maybe,' she said.

Fausto's eyes travelled slowly downwards from her face, seeming to caress her slender neck, her shapely shoulders, the full-blooming softness of her breasts. And

Tanya could not stop the blush that crept betrayingly into her cheeks. She could feel the agitation in her now mounting almost to fever-pitch. Her eyes dropped to her lap. Her mouth had suddenly gone dry.

'Maybe you'll be able to get started on the decorating while I'm gone,' she heard him say. 'I've left a list of useful addresses and phone numbers on your desk. Decorators, suppliers of various sorts. Most of the big ones are in Milan, but there are one or two closer to home that you might try.'

She swallowed hard and nodded, but somehow couldn't bring herself to look at him. She was afraid of what she might see written in his eyes, even more of the message that she feared was scrawled quite unequivocally in hers. 'Good,' she said through lips that felt numb. 'I'd like to make a start on it.'

'OK.' He paused. 'Of course, if you get stuck with anything, do feel free to give Bea a ring. I'm sure she'd be happy to help you out. I've left her number just in case.'

That jolted her. 'I'm sure I can manage without the countess's assistance, thank you.' The angry bitterness in her voice came as a shock as her eyes shot up to mesh with his. She added, embarrassed, 'I'd prefer to do it on my own, if you don't mind.'

'Of course.' Fausto leaned forward in his seat, dropping his strong, tanned hands between his knees, and the dark eyes held a strangely intent expression that belied his conversational tone as he went on, 'If you have to go into Milan for anything and you don't feel like driving there yourself, get Beppe to take you. He knows his way around. Likewise if you want to go to Lugano to visit your father. I've left strict instructions with both Beppe and Emma that they're to take good care of you while I'm away.' And still he went on watching her with that unfathomable expression in his eyes.

Suddenly she couldn't bear it any more. The tension

in her was tightening almost to strangulation point. Abruptly, she stood up, aware that she was trembling almost uncontrollably. 'If that's all, I think I'll go now. I'm very tired.'

'Tanya.' Before she could move, he had risen to his feet and caught her lightly by the arm.

She couldn't speak. Helplessly, she turned to look at him, mute supplication in her eyes. Let me go, please let me go, they begged. But his own eyes answered with a silent no.

For what seemed like an agonised eternity, she stared into their inky depths, dimly aware of the firm, strong arm that stole gently around her waist. His hand reached up to smooth the hair softly from her face, lingering to brush her cheek with a feather-light caress. Tanya's heart was hammering so hard she feared she must surely faint before his lips at last came down on hers and she felt the heat of his body overwhelming her as he drew her close.

His gentleness took her by surprise, for there was none of the harsh ferocity of that former kiss. His mouth's possession of hers was teasing, soft, exploratory, yet erotic almost beyond endurance for all that. Hungry with arousal, her lips parted for him, inviting him to deepen the tantalising exploration of her mouth.

She could feel the hard contours of his body pressing against her thighs as she clung to him, drowning in the tidal wave of her own aching desire. His hand slid gently to her breast, light fingers moulding the full swell of it, his thumb brushing the taut, throbbing peak through the thin, constricting cotton of her blouse. And she could scarcely breathe for the agony of wanting him.

'Tanya.' His voice was husky as he traced a fiery trail of kisses down the softness of her throat, lingering to press his lips on the fluttering pulse above her collarbone. 'I want to make love to you, Tanya,' he whispered tremblingly against her face.

She would gladly have surrendered to him then, she realised with almost shocking certitude. But he drew back and cupped his fingers lightly to her chin. 'But tonight is not the right time. I'm leaving tomorrow morning, early.' And he kissed her softly and pulled her close to him again. 'When I get back.' His eyes held hers, their silent promise echoing the stark commitment of his words. Then he smiled and dropped a teasing kiss on to her nose. 'Promise me you'll still be here when I get back.'

She nodded. 'I'll be here.' She sighed as she leaned her quivering body against his. For suddenly she knew that she would never want to leave.

CHAPTER SEVEN

FORTUNATELY, with the work on the old wash-house to get under way, Tanya had plenty to occupy her mind while Fausto was away. The list of contacts he had left her proved invaluable and, as he had predicted, much of what she required to translate her two-dimensional design sketches into living, three-dimensional reality was readily available from various centres in the area.

Furnishing fabrics, carpets, tiles—and even lamps and various other bits of bric-à-brac—were to be found in elegant abundance in the regional capital of Varese. And, to her delight, just a few kilometres down the road in Ispra she managed to track down a first-class painter and decorator who promised his team would start work on the painting and papering by the end of the week. Even some of the furniture—a couple of beds with their matching commodes—she eventually ordered from a warehouse near Stresa, though the bulk of the furniture, she decided, demanded a visit to the more exclusive manufacturers in Milan. Her days started early and finished late as she buzzed tirelessly around the countryside in the nippy little Alfa Romeo that Fausto had designated for her use, chatting to tilers and plumbers and electricians, searching through acres of chintz and fine wool carpeting, examining shade charts and taking endless measurements.

A few suggestions that Fausto had made, scribbled in the margins of her sketches in his strong, clear hand, she had found to her relief were positive contributions rather than criticisms. 'What about a couple of real oil lamps in the bedrooms?' one of them read. 'I think a group of old family photographs on the wall in the sitting-room would look good,' suggested another. She found the oil lamps, in immaculate brass with their original glass chimneys still intact, in an old antiques shop in the heart of Milan during one of her trips there with Beppe. The family photographs would have to wait for Fausto's return.

But through all the excitement of her frantic activity that absorbed virtually every waking hour of her day, one thought was never far from the forefront of Tanya's consciousness: Fausto, and what would happen when he returned. By day she almost managed for brief periods to push the dark obsession from her mind, but by night, as she lay awake for long hours in her solitary bed, it haunted her. For no longer could she deny the feelings he aroused in her. The aching want, the fierce, sharp keening of desire as she relived again and again those magical, tormented moments with him in the library.

She had wanted him then as she had wanted no man in her life before. As she had never even imagined it was possible to want someone. The persuasive intimacy of that gentle kiss, the sweet, seductive pressure of his body against hers, the warmth, the clean male smell of him, the tantalising touch of his strong hand against her breast had unleashed at last the torrent of emotions she had fought for so long to control. And the stark, new knowledge of the deep and sensual power he exerted over her both thrilled and terrified her.

It had all happened so quickly, so suddenly. In the few, short weeks she had known him she had witnessed so many different and conflicting sides of him that she found it impossible even now to piece together the puzzle that was Fausto Cabrini. He was a man, it seemed, of irreconcilable opposites: one minute hard and ruthless, the next, warm and humane, and rarely, if ever, predictable.

Yet there was one thing about him of which she had always been sure. Fausto Cabrini was a man who knew what he wanted in life—and who, furthermore, was used to getting it. And she shivered, recalling the words he had spoken to her in the library: 'I want to make love to you, Tanya. But tonight is not the right time. When I come back.' Words he had spoken like a vow, as though there was no doubt in his mind that they would be fulfilled. And though she knew that her body wanted him, she felt afraid. For Fausto, making love to her might mean no more than the gratification of a passing whim. For her, a voice deep in her soul kept warning her, it would mean a great deal more than that.

It was not, she knew, simply because he would be the first man to make love to her—though the fact that she felt so eager to surrender her virginity to him was somehow significant enough. It was more, much more, the voice inside her cautioned her. For instinctively she understood that by allowing Fausto to possess her physically she would inevitably allow him to strengthen the hold he already had on her. And that hold, she acknowledged almost resentfully, was already more than powerful enough.

For how long could any relationship between them last? In just a matter of months she would be gone from here—and that would be the end of it. In spite of the aching longing that she felt for him, could she really bear to be just one more conquest on his list?

The lingering question was forced into uncomfortably sharp relief midway through the week when the Countess Bea telephoned. 'Tanya dear, I've just heard through the grapevine that Fausto's in New York. How long will he be gone—do you know?' The purring, feline tones sent an instant shiver of dislike down Tanya's spine. She could picture her curled up, catlike, on her plush divan examining her long, carmine fingernails as she spoke.

'Just for a few days,' Tanya responded woodenly. 'He'll be back at the beginning of next week.' And she felt a faint puff of pleasure in spite of her antipathy. So he hadn't bothered to inform the countess he was going away.

But she was instantly deflated as the countess sighed, 'That's a relief. I was a little worried that he might not be back in time for our dinner date next week.'

Drat the woman! 'Oh, I'm sure he'd make a special point of being back for that,' Tanya managed to force out in a heavily sarcastic tone of voice. It was the first *she'd* heard of any such dinner date. Involuntarily her fingers tightened round the telephone.

The countess responded with a throaty little laugh. 'Wicked of me, I know, to take him away from you again as soon as he gets back. But you really mustn't expect the poor man to think of nothing except work.' Again the laugh. 'Even he needs a little diversion from day-to-day routine. I'm sure you know what I mean, my dear.'

Tanya knew exactly the manner of diversion that the countess had in mind—and she found herself wishing that the receiver she held so tightly in her hand was instead the Countess Bea's pretty litle neck. 'It's so nice to know there's someone like you who has his well-being at heart,' she managed to spit out, only half civilly.

'Oh, believe me, none more than I.' The countess paused. 'So how are you managing in his absence, my dear?'

'Perfectly, thank you.'

'I hope he's left you plenty to keep you occupied?'

'Plenty.' Tanya was loath to mention the wash-house job. The last thing she planned to do was encourage the countess to poke her nose in on that.

But the countess poked her nose in anyway. 'By the way, I hope you're keeping my offer in mind——to give you any help you need with that little decorating job. My late husband, the count, you see, had interests in the furniture trade. I have dozens of contacts. All you have to do is say the word.'

The only word Tanya felt any compulsion to say was no, followed by a swift goodbye. But she told the countess sweetly, 'That's very good of you, I'll let you know.'

'*Bene*. So I'll leave you to get on with your work.' And she paused slightly before purring, 'Be sure to remind Fausto that he and I are having dinner next Friday night. You won't forget, will you, my dear?'

'I won't forget.'

'That's sweet of you. He wouldn't want to miss it, I'm sure. *Addio*—and don't work too hard.'

Tanya banged the receiver down and counted, very slowly, to ten. It was really none of her business, of course, what Fausto's relationship with the countess was. A couple of kisses in the library scarcely endowed her with some sort of territorial rights over the man. Yet the thought of him in the arms of that ridiculous, fawning woman made her feel almost physically sick. Impatiently she pushed the unpleasant thought away, appalled at the strength of feeling that the image had aroused in her, and, with an effort, turned her attention to the somewhat less disturbing task of selecting wallpaper for the wash-house drawing-room.

The painters and decorators were already installed by the time she made her second trip to the Heinrich Castelli Clinic to visit her father, this time accompanied by the ever-obliging Beppe, proudly rigged out in the chauffeur's livery he insisted on wearing on their every trip.

Devlin was looking even better than he had the time before. He had put on more weight and had even, it seemed to Tanya as she talked with him, regained a

measure of his old self-confidence. When she finished
telling him about the wash-house decorating job, he
gave her a conspiratorial wink. 'You're not the only one
who's been keeping busy recently,' he confided, a
mischievous twinkle in the light blue eyes. 'Quite by
chance, I discovered that one of the doctors here is an
aficionado of early eighteenth-century English minia-
tures—and since I happen to know where I can get him
some, it looks like we're back in business again.' He
grinned an almost boyish grin. 'It's only a small
beginning, but I have a feeling it could lead to other
things. You see, there's life in the old dog yet, Tanya.'

She smiled at him in simultaneous pleasure and
concern. 'That's marvellous. I just hope you're not
overdoing things. You've been very ill, remember, and
you've a bit to go before you're fully recovered.'

'I know, I know.' He patted her hand. 'But I owe it to
both of us, as well as to Signor Cabrini, to get myself
back on my feet as soon as possible. And this is the ideal
opportunity. Don't worry,' he added as she started to
protest again, 'I won't overdo it—but you can tell
Signor Cabrini that he can expect the first repayment on
his loan within the next couple of months.'

Tanya shook her head and frowned. The last thing she
wanted to do was discourage her father in his recovery,
but neither did she want to see him risk his health to
repay a loan which to Fausto, on his own admission, was
a mere drop in the ocean. 'Just remember,' she told him,
keeping her tone light, 'the most important thing is that
you get your health back. The loan can wait.'

But Devlin brushed her cautious words aside. 'No, the
loan can't wait. For all our sakes, dealing with that has to
be my first priority.'

Tanya drove back from Lugano with mixed feelings.
Huddled in the back of the air-conditioned Mercedes,
she stared out blankly at the moving landscape and

found herself wondering about the strange quirks of fate that had brought her here—and about the man who suddenly seemed to loom so large in both her own and her father's life. Mere weeks ago he had been a stranger, a name with neither form nor face. All at once and unchallenged he had assumed a fearfully pivotal position in both their lives. And this was only the beginning, she sensed.

According to Tanya's calculations, Fausto was due back some time on Sunday, and as the day approached the tension inside her mounted almost to fever pitch. All day Saturday she could not sit still, shuttling nervously from chore to chore, making the journey from the villa to the wash-house at least a dozen unnecessary times. She was almost worn out by seven o'clock when the workmen finally packed up their gear and left her alone to admire the transformation that their two days' labour had wrought to the freshly painted and papered walls.

'I'm very impressed.'

She spun round startled to find Fausto leaning in the open doorway, watching her. 'You!' was all she could stutter as her heart began pounding crazily against her ribs.

'I decided to come back early. Aren't you pleased?' And he raised a mocking eyebrow at her and smiled as he surveyed the room. 'I have to congratulate you. You haven't wasted any time.'

He was wearing a cream-coloured suit that was slightly crumpled from long hours seated in a plane, and his chin was shadowed by a dark stubble of beard that gave him a faintly roguish look. She stared at him, a sudden helpless longing overwhelming her. She had both ached for and dreaded this moment, and now that it had come she could not move. 'I think they've done a pretty good job.' She could scarcely even bear to look at him.

He nodded. 'Excellent.' Then went on, 'I've asked Emma to delay dinner by half an hour. I want to have a shower and change before we eat. I hope that's OK with you.'

'Of course.' She wondered if she looked as awkward as she felt.

'Have you finished here?' A smile of amusement brushed his lips.

She shifted her eyes abruptly from his face. 'For the moment.'

'In that case let's go.' He led her outside. 'By the way, I think it's time we did something about this path——' indicating the dusty trail that led through the wood back to the house '——I'll arrange for a flagstone path to be laid. It should be possible without too much damage to the trees.' He turned and threw her a teasing grin. 'We can't have you doing any more damage to your feet.'

Her feet were the last thing on Tanya's mind as she nervously followed him back to the house. And, up in her room, as she slipped into a demure white blouse—high-necked, long-sleeved—and a voluminous skirt that covered her knees, she was beginning to wonder quite seriously if she had the nerve to see the evening through. But perhaps, she consoled herself with a determined shrug, she really had nothing to worry about. He had made no move towards her since his return, not even so much as a touch of his hand, and had made not the smallest reference to what had passed between them in the library that night. More than likely, he had quite forgotten it.

His dark eyes told her nothing as he sat down opposite her at the dinner-table. He had shaved and changed into a black silk shirt and slim black trousers that hugged the lean, hard hips. He seemed relaxed, though perhaps a trifle thoughtful, Tanya observed, wishing feverishly that she could read his mind. Her own confused emotions, she supposed, were written as plain as a billboard across her face.

'Did you have a good trip?' she asked somewhat belatedly, abandoning her efforts with the soup. It tasted of nothing to her dry, parched mouth and she was having considerable difficulty in swallowing it.

'It was pretty hectic,' he observed. A curl of dark hair showed at the open neck of his black silk shirt. Tanya jerked her eyes away as he went on, 'Fortunately I managed to get everything I went for done. I'm trying to arrange the transfer of even more of our business interests to Milan. Within the next five years or so the bulk of Cabrini Industries will be operational from here. Which will thankfully mean fewer trips to New York for me.' He smiled a faintly weary smile. 'It's a place I prefer to spend as little time as possible in—even though I was born and brought up there.'

'I've never been to New York,' Tanya said, really just for something to say. Her eyes kept drifting to his mouth, half hypnotised by the oddly sensuous movements of his lips as he spoke, and it was taking all her determination just to keep dragging them away. What the devil had got into her? she asked herself impatiently. She was allowing her physical attraction to the man to become an obsession. She would be caught in a web of her own weaving if she didn't watch out.

He had leaned his elbows on the table and was watching her. 'I'll take you some day,' he offered with a smile, then added lightly, seemingly unaware of the flush of nervous colour his words had brought to Tanya's cheeks, 'Maybe you'll be like Renata and love the place.'

She forced herself to meet his eyes. 'Did you see Renata while you were in New York?' Deliberately side-stepping the subtle implication of his previous remark, suppressing the flutter of excitement it had so foolishly awakened in her heart.

'We had dinner together a couple of times. She's very well, as usual. She sends you her love and looks forward to seeing you in a few weeks' time.'

'Renata's coming here?' The thought of her old friend arriving on the scene was a warming thought. Perhaps, Tanya found herself daring to hope, Renata's presence might restore an element of order and normality to the emotional chaos that was currently afflicting her.

'She always spends some time in Europe at this time of year. And of course she wouldn't miss the party for the world.' The well shaped lips twisted in a brief, wry smile. 'By the way, it's time you and I started to get this party organised. We usually hold it the last week of July before everyone takes off for the August holidays. That doesn't leave us very much time.'

'No.' For some reason, the prospect of this party filled Tanya with no enthusiasm at all. 'That reminds me,' she went on, a slight edge to her voice, 'your friend the countess telephoned.'

'Bea?' The dark brows lifted, interested.

'She was worried that you might not be back in time for your dinner date.'

He smiled one of his irritating smiles. 'No doubt you set her mind at rest?'

'I told her I was sure you wouldn't miss it for the world.'

'How right you are.' He poured more wine for both of them. 'And what else did my friend the countess have to say?'

'Not much.' If he was deliberately trying to wind her up, he was making a very good job of it indeed. What little self-possession she could have put her name to at the start of the meal seemed to be evaporating now before her eyes. He was so damned sure of himself, and there was she sitting feeling like a schoolgirl with a crush. 'She renewed her generous offer to put me in touch with her many contacts in the furniture trade.'

'And you immediately sent her packing, I suppose?' He was leaning back in his chair, watching her with a bantering smile.

'I refrained from leaping at her offer, if that's what you mean. I assure you, I don't need her help.'

'Just as long as you were polite to her.'

Tanya felt her spine stiffen aggressively. 'Is it really so important to you whether I was polite or not?'

He looked at her for a long, hard moment before answering. 'Yes, Tanya, I'm afraid it is,' he said at last. 'Aside from being a personal friend, Bea is a client of mine—and, whatever your private feelings towards her might be, I expect you, as my assistant, to treat her with civility. As I would expect you to treat any other client, come to that.' An ominous glint shone in the dark eyes.

Bastard! And more fool her for stupidly mentioning the countess's phone call in the first place, she thought. 'I don't need any lectures from you on how I should conduct myself—whether with your clients or your mistresses!' she stormed. 'As your so-called *assistant*——' she managed a sarcastic little laugh '—I am perfectly aware of my inferior position here. You're the one who calls all the shots. Don't worry, I haven't forgotten that!'

'I'm glad to hear it.' His lips were a thin white line as he stared ferociously across the table at her. 'At least we've managed to get one thing straight.'

Tanya barely touched the rest of her meal. She was burning inside with a bitter fury that was directed as much at herself as at the darkly composed figure seated opposite her. What a fool she had been to imagine that this man's heart was made of anything but stone, that he

might be more than the soulless tyrant she had originally
taken him for. And a throb of hurt and disappointment
clutched her heart. He cared for no one. Yet, thank God,
she bitterly admonished herself, she had come to her
senses again before it was too late.

She was only half listening when he instructed Emma
to serve them coffee out on the terrace.

'I think we could both use a breath of fresh air.'

She realised belatedly that the remark had been
addressed to her. Her eyes snapped up, resentment still
sparking in their tawny depths. 'Whatever you like,' she
shrugged ill-humouredly. 'It's all the same to me.'

Heels clicking defiantly against the dark ceramic tiles,
she followed him on to the terrace and crossed to lean
against the parapet, very deliberately turning her back to
him. Behind her she heard Emma lay out the coffee
things on one of the slatted wooden tables, then
discreetly take her leave of them.

A silence descended. Tanya remained motionless,
staring unseeingly into the night, feeling the faint breeze
gently fan her cheeks and wondering how long he was
going to stand there watching her. For, though she
would not turn to look at him, she could feel the dark
eyes probing like sharp fingers into her back.

'Black or white?' A sudden movement glimpsed from
the corner of her eye as he lifted the silver coffee-pot.

'Black, please.' And still she did not turn her head.

'I'll leave it here.' A spoon clicked against the
porcelain, then there was silence again.

The sky was filled with stars. The moon hung low.
Out in the distance, beyond the trees, she caught the
occasional restless glimmer of the lake. It was a perfect
summer's evening, she reflected bitterly. Or might have
been.

'Your coffee's getting cold.'

She hadn't even heard him move, but as she swung

round, startled, he was standing at the parapet beside her, mere inches away. She fought the sudden impulse to back away from him. 'Let it,' she retorted, angry that she had let him take her by surprise. 'I don't really want it anyway.'

He was standing very still, the dark eyes scrutinising her face. 'Don't you think you're behaving a little childishly?' he asked.

She glared at him, daring him to move any closer to her. As it was, he was already standing far too near. So near she could hear the quiet sound of his breathing, feel the masculine warmth of him prickling against her skin. She scrambled in her mind for something to say, but her mind had suddenly gone blank.

'Don't spoil things, Tanya. We've got nothing to fight about.'

Her spoil things! *He* was the one who had ruined everything! She turned on him. 'Why are you always so——?'

But he stopped her short, his lips descending with ruthless precision to smother her protests with a kiss. He tasted of coffee, warm and sweet, as his arms slipped firmly around her waist, crushing her body against his, defying her feeble efforts to free herself from him. Not that she really had much heart to struggle anyway. At the very first touch of him, her anger had dissolved, replaced by another emotion, less familiar, but infinitely more powerful.

She gulped for air as he released her momentarily. 'Why am I always so what?' he teased.

'So utterly impossible!' Her body suddenly felt so weak that if he were to step back there and then and let her go, she knew for certain that she would fall.

But he had no intention of letting her go. His arms were still clasped tightly around her waist. 'Am I?' And he kissed her nose. 'I missed you, you know. Did you miss me?'

She frowned. 'Maybe.' The overwhelming nearness of him took her breath away.

He smiled. 'I've always hated indecision,' he said. 'Let's see if I can coax a more positive answer out of you.' And he lowered his mouth to cover hers again, plundering sweet kisses from her trembling lips, sending shivers of raw excitement racing down her spine. She could not resist. Helplessly, she raised one hand to bury her fingers in the thick dark hair, her need for him clamouring through her body like a storm as her lips responded to the ravaging urgency of his.

His voice was ragged with emotion when he spoke. 'That's better.' Then, wordlessly, he took her by the hand, led her across the terrace and through the empty dining-room into the hall. At the foot of the big staircase he paused and planted a soft kiss on her lips before lifting her bodily into his arms, almost as though she weighed nothing at all. And started the long ascent to the upper floor.

She couldn't breathe. She closed her eyes and pressed her face against his neck, wondering in panic if she still had time to change her mind, knowing in her deepest soul that nothing in the world could make her change it now. And she shivered as they reached the top of the stairs, clung tightly to him as he carried her with swift, sure strides down the wide and seemingly endless corridor.

She didn't open her eyes again until they were inside his room. A big room, she registered numbly, lit by a single shaded lamp that stood on the table next to the vast expanse of bed. The door closed behind them and her heart almost stopped. Her body felt suddenly nerveless in his arms. The hammering in her chest had grown so loud she wondered it didn't fill the room.

He laid her gently on the gold silk coverlet, leaned over her and softly brushed her lips with his. Then he lowered himself gently alongside her on the bed and caressed the side of her face with his fingertips. 'Don't be afraid, Tanya,' he whispered with another kiss as his fingers lightly stroked the warm skin of her throat. 'Trust me.'

She bit her lip and gazed helplessly into the deep, dark eyes. Whatever reservations she had harboured in her heart were all forgotten now, swept to oblivion by the sudden, thundering demands of her body's need for him.

Unhurriedly, he started to undo the buttons of her high-necked blouse, then deftly slid his hand behind her to release the fastening of her lace-cupped bra. As the full, proud breasts spilled free, he cupped them softly in his hands and lowered his face to drop sweet kisses into the scented valley between. His lips burned like fire against her skin, and the slow, circling movement of his palms was a delicious torment, urging the rosy buds of her nipples into stiff, hard peaks. And she gasped as he drew the swollen flesh into his mouth, teasing gently with his tongue, whipping her senses to a pitch of arousal beyond pleasure, approaching a torment of intensity almost like pain.

Then his mouth returned to hers, moist and demanding, coaxing her eager lips apart, and she found herself responding without reticence to the silken invasion of his tongue. And all the while, his hands circled the bare flesh of her breats, the brush of his palms against their aching peaks sending swift tremors of excitement coursing through her, making her groan with ecstasy deep in her throat.

Without haste, his hand slid down towards her waist, caressing every curve and contour on the way, and she felt the loose skirt slip easily from her hips and the sharp thrill of anticipation as his fingers eased the lacy briefs away.

He paused then to gaze down at her nakedness, a look of veneration clouding the dark eyes. 'You're beautiful, Tanya.' He kissed her again as he swiftly unbuttoned the black silk shirt, let it slide from his shoulders to the floor, unhooked the leather belt at his waist and quickly freed himself of his remaining clothes.

She watched him as though mesmerised, then raised one tentative hand to touch the bronzed, hair-roughened chest. He was magnificently built, lean yet deeply muscled, the shoulders broad and powerful, the plane of his stomach hard and flat. He took her hand, let her fingers brush the flat nubs of his nipples, then gently lowered himself on top of her.

He kissed her again, this time with hungry urgency, and she trembled as his hand moved down between her thighs, touching the moist, most secret parts of her with infinite, tantalising delicacy. Involuntarily, her body arched as his fingers gently coaxed and stroked, driving her senses to an unknown edge of ecstasy, sending shockwaves of desire pulsing through her throbbing flesh.

She sobbed as he gently eased her legs apart and she felt the hard male arousal of him press against her thigh. Then she clung to him as he moved in closer to appease the hunger he had so masterfully aroused. She gasped in momentary pain as his hardness penetrated her soft flesh, then sank back, lost in spiralling pleasure as he moved inside her, the gentle rhythm of his passion carrying her relentlessly towards release.

They lay quietly together for a long time afterwards, their bodies still joined, like two spent craft washed up on the shore after the storm. And as Tanya gazed down wonderingly at the dark head lying so peacefully against her breast, she felt an unfamiliar ache of tenderness clutch at her heart. He had been all that she could have dreamed of, and much more. He had drawn her along that unfamiliar path with gentle, caring expertise, making each unforgettable step an experience of exquisite delight. And for that she felt intensely grateful to him.

Yet beneath that gentle lover lurked a man of steel, a man who would never allow his sensitivities to gain the upper hand. She knew the cold, hard, ruthless side of him too well to be blinded by the brief, tender interlude they had just shared. And she reached out wistfully to touch the dark, soft hair. It had seemed, while he was making love to her, as though their very souls were reaching out to touch, as though all the barriers between the two of them were suddenly torn down. But it was not so, she found herself reflecting with a sharp twinge of regret. He remained what he had always been to her—a man of bitter, irreconcilable complexity. A man, perhaps, whom she would never understand.

And she sighed as he stirred and slipped away from her, raising his head to gaze at her with deep and penetrating eyes. Then his arms reached out and drew her close as he kissed the damp hair from her face. 'So you were a virgin, after all. I thought as much.' He kissed the two spots of colour that had risen to her cheeks. 'Don't blush, Tanya. I consider it an honour to have been the first.'

And I am honoured that you were. The words went through her head but she left them unsaid. The less he knew of the feelings he aroused in her the safer she would feel. Never would she let him guess the strength of the power he had over her.

He kissed her again, then leaned past her to the little table at the side of the bed and pulled open a drawer. 'I brought you something from New York.' And he opened his hand to reveal a small, square, leatherbound box. He held it out to her. 'See if it fits.'

She took the box with trembling hands, knowing what it must contain. She lifted the lid with racing heart, hardly daring to glance at him. It was a perfect diamond solitaire, at least three carats, she estimated, judging by its size. As big as a pea, flashing rainbow colours at her from its satin-lined bed.

'Fausto, I——' She turned to look at him in numb astonishment.

He took her free hand in his and raised it softly to his lips. 'I want to marry you, Tanya,' he said. 'I want you to be my wife.'

CHAPTER EIGHT

'I CAN'T.' Tanya's fingers were still trembling as she snapped the box shut, and sudden helpless tears were brimming in her eyes. Shakily, she made to hand it back to him.

But firm brown fingers closed over her hand. 'The ring is yours, Tanya, whatever you decide.' And he kissed her arm, sending helpless shudders up her spine. 'I know I've probably taken you by surprise. You need a little time to think.'

She stared at him dumbly, biting her lip. The torrent of emotions raging through her at that moment made no sense at all. She wanted him so badly—God, how she wanted him. Yet she could not bring herself to say yes, did not dare to throw herself into his arms and surrender to him totally, tell him that she loved him, yet feared him still. For it was fear, she realised, that held her back. Fear that her total capitulation would destroy her utterly. He had possessed her body, even her heart—but her soul, fragile as it felt as she knelt there at his side, was still her own. 'Why do you want to marry me?' she asked at last.

His hand caressed her shoulder. 'Why do you think I want to marry you? Because I love you, of course.'

She shook her head. 'No,' she said. 'That can't be true.'

'Why not?' He caught her chin lightly between his fingers and forced her to look at him.

'What about all the other women in your life?' she asked.

Fausto smiled. Don't worry, I'd be happy to give them up for you.'

Tanya took a deep breath. 'Even the countess?' she asked.

He leaned his dark head against the pillow, watching her. 'Aren't you prepared to leave me even one?'

His words were like a knife-wound in her side. Was he joking or was he serious? It hurt almost to look at him.

He reached out and brushed the back of her hand with his fingertips. 'But that's not the reason you won't say yes. Is it, Tanya?' And the dark eyes seemed to bore down to her very soul. 'Do you love me?'

Helplessly she closed her eyes. How could she ever begin to explain to him the feelings that she felt? The depth and intensity of emotion he aroused in her was something that stirred her to the very foundations of her being—but was it love? Surely love was a sweet and gentle thing, not this raging torrent that seemed to consume her and tear apart her peace of mind. Love was reassuring, kind—not the terrifying torment that she felt. And she forced herself to breathe deeply and folded her arms protectively around herself. No, what she felt for Fausto could not be love. This dark obsession could never bring her happiness. If she submitted, it would only end up by destroying her. For a long moment she held her breath. 'I don't think so,' she said at last.

Fausto slid silently from the bed. 'Think about my offer anyway,' he said. 'I'll know your answer when I see you wear the ring.' He paused on his way over to the bathroom and turned to her with a wry smile. 'But don't keep me waiting too long, Tanya. I'll expect a decision, one way or the other, by the end of the month.'

She could have said no then, of course, made her decision on the spot, ended the agony before it had begun. But she did not. Could not. Though she feared what might become of her should she capitulate, she dreaded even more the thought of losing him.

Yet how typical of the man, she thought resentfully. He had set her a deadline as though it were some day-today business contract he was negotiating. Which, she reflected ruefully, was probably exactly what it was to him. For, despite what he had told her, she could not accept that he really loved her at all. Those were just words he had spoken because he thought they sounded right. He was probably incapable of loving anyone—but had decided, for reasons she did not even attempt to fathom, that she would make him a suitable wife. He had made his offer, and now her answer—one way or another, as he had so dispassionately put it himself—was required within a fixed and reasonable period of time.

Many times over the next few days she found herself wishing that she was capable of viewing the matter in as detached a frame of mind as he so evidently did.

They had never made love again since that first night. He had barely come near her. And she, for her part, had not encouraged him. Their relationship seemed to be down-spiralling into a sort of psychological waiting game, with neither one apparently prepared to make the move or say the word that would release them from the suffocating deadlock in which they both now found themselves.

It was on the Friday, just under a week after Fausto's proposal, that the inevitable explosion finally occurred. The seeds were sown as they were sharing an uneasy lunch out on the terrace. With an air of almost callous indifference to her sensibilities, Fausto suddenly remarked, 'I expect you're remembering that I'm dining with Bea tonight?'

She hadn't forgotten. It was just one among dozens of niggling anxieties that had been preying on her mind for days. 'Of course not.' But she had been praying that he might have cancelled it.

'Good.' He dropped his eyes down to his plate again, summarily dismissing her. 'I'll be leaving here about eight.'

'I'm not invited, I suppose?' It was an empty

question. She knew the answer before the words had left her lips. But she hadn't expected him to phrase it quite so brutally.

'Most definitely not. The last thing I want is to spend an evening watching you two at each other's throats.'

She winced—but she knew that wasn't the real reason. He really just wanted to have the countess to himself. 'So it's pleasure rather than business, I presume?'

His eyes snapped up. 'Why do you ask?'

'No reason.'

'Good. Then there's no reason why I should answer you.' He looked her straight in the eye then, and there was malice there. 'You and I have no commitment to one another as far as I know. I don't go asking you about your personal affairs.'

Tanya hated him for that. She hated him for deliberately hurting her, and for the way, over the past few days, he had never once let his composure slip. And it struck her again that marriage, to Fausto Cabrini, was probably just another business deal. And that she— presentable, intelligent and young enough to bear him many heirs—had apparently fitted the bill as a suitable candidate. With the additional bonus, of course, that she had been a virgin. For she had not forgotten how his proposal had come only after he had personally satisfied himself on that particular point.

He had once confided to her, had he not, that he had neither conscience, soul nor heart? At least she would never be able to say that she hadn't been warned.

It was really too much, though, to expect her just to stay docilely at home while he went traipsing off to dinner with that tramp. That was surely the ultimate in deliberate offensiveness. Almost more than flesh and blood could bear.

She had dinner alone on a tray in her room and spent the rest of the evening, in a kind of orgy of masochism, torturing herself with images of Fausto and the countess on their dinner date. The two of them sharing some secluded table, gazing lustfully across the candlelight into each other's eyes. The countess, of course, tricked out like the vulgar little vamp she was, her gaudy mouth purring rapturously at every smart remark her escort made, her matching gaudy fingernails clutching possessively at his sleeve. And he, in his vanity, would be lapping it up.

About ten o'clock, she went downstairs to the drawing-room and poured herself an Armagnac. It failed, however, to blunt her imagination as she had hoped it would. On the contrary, it simply seemed to fire the more lurid corners of her brain. She was forced to pour herself another one to blot the evil visions out.

The phone rang. She struggled to her feet and raced across to answer it. Maybe it was Fausto calling to apologise.

It was not. 'Tanya! Tanya, sweetheart, don't be alarmed, but I'm calling from a friend's house in Luxembourg!'

Tanya frowned as she instantly recognised her father's voice. 'Luxembourg! What in the name of heaven are you doing there?'

'I told you not to get alarmed,' Devlin continued on a blithely cheerful note. 'I'm fine. I discharged myself from the clinic this afternoon and I've come here to visit an old business chum of mine. Got a bit of a deal brewing, you see. I'm off to Stuttgart tomorrow, then Paris for a couple of days. I'll phone you again in a week or so's time.' There was a sudden crackling on the line.

'Father, Father ...' It was all too much to take in at one go. She clutched the receiver anxiously to her ear. 'Tell me what's going on? Why did you leave the clinic? Why didn't you let me know that you were going to discharge yourself?'

But the line had gone bad. Through the interference she heard him say, 'Don't worry. I'll call you from

Paris.' Then the line went dead.

She sat down again and cradled her drink between trembling hands. What on earth was going on? First, Fausto abandoned her to go off and have dinner with the countess in Milan, then Devlin phoned out of the blue from Luxembourg and casually entreated her not to be alarmed! Her whole world was suddenly falling apart at the seams.

She downed the drink and got up stiffly to pour herself another one. It was all Fausto's fault, of course. His fault that she was suffering such agonies; his fault, too, that her father had made this rash and foolish move. And what did he care? Nothing. While the world was rattling down about her ears, he was making love to the countess. She glanced at her watch. It was almost twelve. That was probably precisely what he was doing now.

By the time she at last heard his key in the lock, a little after one o'clock, she had worked herself up into an emotional ferment. As his footsteps sounded across the hall, uncaring and briskly confident, she was ready to demolish him in one go. He appeared in the drawing-room doorway, a tall figure in a white jacket and black trousers—and, in spite of her anger, her heart turned over at the sight of him.

'What are you doing up at this time of night?' He was wearing no tie and the top few buttons of his white silk shirt were open. Had he dressed in a hurry? Tanya asked herself.

'Waiting for you, as a matter of fact.'

He seemed to consider her answer. 'Well, that's uncommonly decent of you.' He leaned against the door-frame with a self-congratulatory smile. 'Since you're so interested, I had a lovely time. Bea sends you her love, by the way.'

'You may have need of that particular commodity. I don't.' She stared back at him ungraciously, her eyes raking his face for tell-tale lipstick smudges, her nostrils sniffing the air for the lingering give-away of female scent. She could divine neither, though she found no solace in the fact. Fausto Cabrini, she knew, was much too clever to be foiled by such crude detection work.

He dislodged himself from the doorway, crossed to the drinks table without looking at her and poured a small measure of what was left of the Armagnac. 'You've been knocking it back a bit,' he said.

'And what else was I supposed to do? Sit here with my macramé while you were having a night out on the town?' It was meant to sound scathing, but it only came out sounding peeved.

He swirled the amber-coloured liquid round in his glass and threw her a darkly reproving look. 'What you do in your own time, Tanya, is really no concern of mine. As I pointed out to you already today, in matters private you are not accountable to me—and I, most definitely, am not accountable to you.'

She glared at him. 'Don't worry, I have no wish to know what you and your precious countess have been up to till this hour.' The anger inside her was growing so fierce it seemed to burn a hole right through her abdomen. 'But I thought you might be interested to know that my father telephoned tonight. From *Luxembourg*,' she emphasised.

He frowned. 'What's he doing there?'

'Some wild business scheme, I understand. He's discharged himself from the clinic.' She spat the words at him like an accusation, her lips twisting bitterly around each angry syllable. 'He's worried about paying back that wretched loan of yours.'

A crease appeared between the jet-black brows. 'Where is he staying? Did he tell you that?'

'I've no idea. We were cut off before I had a chance to ask him anything. At a friend's house, he said, though he didn't say whose. He's off to Stuttgart tomorrow. And Paris after that.'

Fausto let slip a colourful oath before crossing quickly to the phone. He laid down his drink and snatched the receiver up.

'Who are you calling?' Tanya asked as she watched him quickly punch some numbers in.

'The clinic.'

'At this hour?'

'My dear,' he told her with an arid smile, 'for the fees I pay, I expect service right round the clock.' He turned his back and began to speak in rapid Italian to someone at the other end.

Tanya stared dolefully into her half-empty glass. Why hadn't she thought of phoning Switzerland? Then she remembered. Ah yes, the Armagnac. Disconsolately she laid her glass down on the coffee-table in front of her.

A moment later, it seemed, he was standing just a couple of feet away. 'The clinic confirms that your father discharged himself just after lunch this afternoon. It was against their advice—they would have preferred him to stay on for another couple of weeks—but, all the same, I don't think we should be too concerned. The senior consultant I spoke to assured me he's well on the road to a full recovery. As long as he's sensible and keeps taking the medication he's been prescribed, he should be perfectly OK.'

As he came to the end of his calm recitation, Tanya fixed him with a resentful stare. 'And I suppose you would call rushing around all over Europe being sensible?' He was always so sure of himself! So absolutely and infuriatingly in control!

'I can only repeat what the doctor said.' There was an unmistakable edge of warning in his voice. 'I can appreciate that you're upset, but remember your father's a grown man with enough intelligence to know what his physical limitations are. I'm sure he won't take any foolish risks.'

'Oh, is that so? And what would you know about what

my father's likely to do? You don't even know him. You don't even give a damn for him, so why pretend?' She could hardly contain the irrational fury that was raging through her now. 'You didn't even care for your own father!' she accused. 'You told me so yourself! You don't really care for anyone, do you?'

He hadn't moved, but the tension she could sense in him was almost overpowering. The muscles around his mouth and jaw were fiercely clenched. His eyes burned like black coals in his face. 'I wouldn't advise you to pursue that line of talk with me,' he advised, the words ground out harshly through tight-set lips. 'You're behaving hysterically. I suggest you calm yourself. Right now.'

Somewhere in the back of her fevered and alcohol-distorted brain she knew that he was right. She was over-reacting, succumbing to the intolerable tensions of the past few days. But the urge to defy him was uncontrollable. With a sob of bitter frustration, she reached out and swept the half-empty glass of Armagnac from the tabletop with the back of her hand. 'Damn you!' she screamed as it shattered into fragments at his feet. 'Why couldn't you just stay out of my life?'

Before she knew what was happening, he had grabbed her roughly by both shoulders and hauled her unceremoniously to her feet. 'You little vixen!' he gritted, shaking her. 'How dare you behave like a spoiled child. Stop it this minute or I'll——'

'You'll what?' she challenged recklessly, refusing to flinch from the passion of anger that had gathered deep in his eyes. 'Will you beat me into submission? Turn on the bully-boy tactics again? I wouldn't put it past you!'

'And you might be right!' For a moment, the expression on the strongly chiselled features was almost dangerous. But the moment passed. 'Is this little exhibition out of genuine concern for your father——' he allowed a small but significant pause before continuing '—or, because, I had dinner with Bea tonight?'

'I wouldn't care if you had dinner with that silly bloody woman every night!'

'I see.' He smiled a faintly triumphant smile and thrust her back into her seat again. 'Such jealousy is really rather flattering, you know.'

She threw him a look of total dislike, hating the craven way she had revealed herself to him. 'You bastard!' she spat at him between her teeth. 'I hate your guts!'

The tall, dark figure continued to stand there, watching her, the expression on his face unreadable. Then, 'Goodnight, Tanya,' he said at last. He turned and walked out of the room.

Tanya couldn't sleep at all after she had gone to bed. Long after the helpless storm of tears had subsided, she tossed and turned. Far from relieving all the pent-up emotions that had been simmering inside, her outburst had simply brought them to the boil. She felt ashamed, confused, resentful, and totally at odds to understand the tumult of conflicting passions that were tearing her apart. The last, slender thread of her control, it seemed, was finally snapping.

She stared into the darkness, lonely and afraid, and wondered what on earth was happening to her. Never—not even in the dark days when her mother had died, nor more recently when Devlin himself had been so close to death—had she experienced the desolation that engulfed her now. It was no good. She had to speak to somebody.

She sat up abruptly, switched on the light, and stared for a seemingly endless moment at the blue phone on the table by the bed. Then she snatched up the receiver, held her breath and resolutely punched the number—nine—that connected with Fausto's room.

Her heart was racing madly as she listened to the ringing tone. What on earth was she going to say to him when he finally answered? And, more to the point, how was he going to react to her waking him like this in the middle of the night?

He would probably be furious, she reasoned, remembering the incandescent, white-hot rage that had burned in the dark eyes earlier. And it was she who had provoked that fury, after all, with those cruel accusations that she regretted now. What she had said about him and his father, she realised now in her sobered state, had been low and utterly despicable. A confidence betrayed and turned against the one who, in trust, had confided it. He would surely never forgive her for that. In fact, it was presumptuous in the extreme to expect any kind of sympathy from him at all.

Suddenly abhorring the rash and foolish impulse that had made her even think of reaching for the phone, she clamped the receiver sharply down again and fell back against the pillows, trembling. Perhaps, she thought dully, a shower might do something to restore some fragment of her sanity. A nice cold, invigorating shower to sluice away the gremlins that had gathered in her head.

Shakily she slid from the bed and pulled the flimsy, damp nightdress over her head. She glanced quickly at her watch on the bedside table before starting across the deep-pile carpet to the bathroom. It was half past three. Thank God she hadn't wakened him.

'You rang?'

Her heart lurched as she swung round to find him standing in the doorway watching her. She felt herself blush from the roots of her hair to the soles of her feet as his eyes travelled wantonly over her nakedness, pausing to linger provocatively on the full, high breasts, the slender waist, the silken mound between her thighs. 'Fausto, I——' She struggled for words to defend herself, to explain. But no words came.

Silently, he closed the door and came towards her, an expression of ironical amusement on his face. He was wearing only a short blue towelling robe, loosely tied about his hips. 'You wanted me for something?' he enquired, arching a mocking eyebrow as he spoke.

She backed away and hastily snatched the discarded nightdress from the floor, clutching it to her to conceal her nakedness. 'I couldn't sleep,' she protested hotly, knowing how feeble it must sound. 'I wanted to talk to you—that's all.' Her mouth felt dry and her heart was hammering uncomfortably against her ribs.

'To talk?' He surveyed her with a coolly disbelieving eye. 'And what particular subject matter did you have in mind?'

The tawny eyes flashed at him indignantly. 'Not what you seem to think,' she rebuked him sharply, then added on a note of appeasement, 'I wanted to apologise.' Perhaps now he would go.

But he didn't go—and, in spite of her embarrassment, Tanya didn't really want him to. 'You mean to tell me you were racked with such remorse that your apology couldn't wait till morning?' came the mildly taunting response. 'I find that somewhat difficult to believe, dear Tanya. Touching, of course, but hardly credible.'

He pulled her roughly to him then, and the blood was thundering in her veins as his mouth ground down on hers with bruising intensity, hungrily prising her lips apart. The nightgown was snatched from her flimsy grasp as his hands reached for her naked breasts, fingers probing the already hardening peaks in an urgent, almost peremptory caress. She half stumbled as he backed her towards the bed, and she wanted to cry out as she felt the robe slip from his shoulders to the floor. But she had no will to resist him, she acknowledged helplessly as the answering clamour of her own senses drowned her unspoken protests and she sank beneath him on to the tumbled bed.

'This is what you wanted, Tanya, isn't it?'

She could feel the weight of his body pressing down

on hers, the sharp caress of his hair-roughened chest against her naked breasts, and she could not deny that what he said was true. She wanted him more than anything.

'Tell me you want me, Tanya,' he growled thickly against her ear, his hands moving downwards to caress her thighs. 'I can feel that you want me. Tell me that you do.'

In trembling response her arms wound tightly round his neck, as though she might never want to let him go, and the words fell like a sob from her lips when at last she whispered, 'I want you.'

His mouth closed down on hers again as he eased her aching thighs apart, but though she hungered to feel his body part of hers he did not enter her. Instead, he let his fingers play a sensual, tatalising magic on her, stroking, caressing, sending warm, pulsating tremors of pleasure coursing through her, making her gasp at the intimate mastery of his touch. Then her fingers knotted in his hair and her back arched to the gathering passion that suddenly exploded, sharp and sweet, throughout her entire being.

A moment later his arms released her and he rolled away from her on to his back. She felt suddenly cold, and reached out her hand to draw him back to her again, but Fausto had already risen from the bed. She watched in silent numbness as he pulled on his robe, then stooped to brush her lips briefly with his before quickly snapping off the bedside light. 'Sleep now, Tanya,' was all he said. And a moment later the door clicked softly as he left the room.

Tanya lay for a long time after he had gone, staring into the emptiness that suddenly surrounded her. Her body felt limp, all emotion spent, and she shivered as she pulled the covers over her. She felt cheated somehow— or that she had cheated him. She was not sure. But the technical fulfilment of her own body's needs was not

enough. What she had been craving so desperately was a
final joining together of the two of them—heart, body
and soul. And he had offered none of these. With a bitter
sob she clutched the pillow to her face and wept.

A kind of numbness descended on Tanya after that. A
blessing, she supposed bleakly, compared with the
agony of indecision and jealousy that had previously
tormented her. Now she could neither feel nor think at
all. Her mind, her very senses, seemed blanked in a sort
of fog, though the dull ache in her heart stirred painfully
whenever Fausto was around. Still, there was one
positive side to their recent, disquieting intimacy, she
told herself. At least this time she need have no fear of
pregnancy. She somehow doubted she would be lucky
on that score a second time.

Fausto continued to act as though nothing had
happened, though she sensed somehow that he was
watching her. The dark eyes seemed to follow her from
room to room, and often, as they lunched or dined
together at the house, she would glance up unexpectedly
to find him gazing at her face. Yet he said nothing to
reveal what thoughts were passing through his head.

It was a week or so later, as she was returning from a
quick trip to Varese to pick up a couple of things for the
old wash-house, that she found him waiting for her out
in the forecourt in front of the villa. She parked the Alfa
in its customary place and climbed out, aware that her
legs had suddenly turned to cotton wool. What did he
want now? she wondered wretchedly, trying to still the
sudden, senseless throbbing in her breast.

He came towards her with an easy stride, hands
thrust deep in his trouser pockets, an indecipherable
expression on his sun-bronzed face. He said, 'Your
father rang while you were out.'

'Oh.' She tried to keep the disappointment that she
felt from showing in her eyes. Her father's promised

phone call was the only thing, amidst her current mood of gloom, that she had actually been looking forward to. 'What did he say?' she asked, following him across the forecourt to the house.

'He was calling from Paris. He sounded fine.' The dark eyes swivelled round to look at her, seeming to probe her features for some response. But she stared impassively back at him as he went on, 'I told him I'd phoned the clinic and what the doctor said about him having to take things relatively easy for a while. He told me to tell you not to worry and that he's not forgetting to take his pills.' A brief smile softened the harsh lines of his face as he paused in the doorway watching her. 'He sends you his love and says he's looking forward to seeing you in a few days' time. He's promised to come to the party and maybe stay on for a day or two afterwards.'

'He's coming here?' Tanya's eyes lit up and relief tinged with a vague anxiety surged through her as she took in the unexpected piece of news. Relief that she would see him soon; anxiety for what his state of health might prove to be. But at least she would have the opportunity now to try to dissuade him from his recklessly ill-advised activities, perhaps even talk him into going back to the clinic in Lugano for a while.

'And Renata called just after your father.' Fausto's voice cut sharply through her thoughts. 'She's arriving some time on Friday afternoon.'

'And my father? When will he be here?' she questioned abruptly, her eyes darting upwards to meet his.

A faintly ironic smile twisted fleetingly at his lips as he answered her. 'I told you, he'll be here for the party—which,' he added with coldly significant emphasis as he moved aside at last to let her pass into the hall, 'I seem to recall we've planned for the last day of the month.'

As she hurried past him the words sent an icy shiver

down Tanya's spine. The last day of the month. The deadline. And now it was only four short days away.

Renata's arrival the day before the party was as welcome as a rainbow after a thunderstorm. Bright, full of colour and somehow reassuring, Tanya found herself musing as the three of them sat down to dinner together on Friday night.

Inevitably, the conversation turned to the subject of the impending party. 'I have to get myself a new dress,' Renata announced, helping herself to a generous spoonful of wild strawberries. Then she laughed out loud at the bemused expression on her brother's face. 'I know what you're thinking, Fausto dear, but I honestly haven't got a thing to wear.' She popped one of the strawberries into her mouth and turned to Tanya with a smile. 'First thing tomorrow morning, *cara*, you and I will take a trip into Milan and treat ourselves to something really extravagant.' And she glanced across at her brother with a mischievous wink. 'Fausto will pay.'

Tanya blushed uncomfortably. What she was to wear for the party was something that had never really crossed her mind. Her choice of attire for the ordeal that she saw ahead had scarcely seemed to matter. She had vaguely supposed that she would borrow something of Renata's, as she had done on several occasions now when accompanying Fausto on his business dinners in Milan, but now she found herself totally at a loss.

Renata almost seemed to read her mind. 'Don't tell me you were planning to wear one of those old things upstairs?' she exclaimed, aghast. 'No, no. You must have something really special for tomorrow night. Consider it a well earned bonus for all the hard work you've done for my brother. I think it's the very least you deserve for putting up with him for all those weeks,' she ended with a teasing smile.

'But I couldn't possibly accept——' Tanya started to protest.

Her voice trailed off as Renata cut in adamantly, 'Nonsense!' Then turned to Fausto for support. 'Tell her not to be silly. Of course she must have a new dress.'

'Of course she must,' he agreed at once, the dark eyes brooking no argument. 'In fact, I absolutely insist on it.'

'So it's agreed!' Renata grinned triumphantly and popped another strawberry into her mouth. 'I'll tell Beppe to be ready to drive us into Milan tomorrow morning at nine o'clock sharp.'

After a morning spent scouring some of the most exclusive dress shops in Milan, Tanya found herself wondering if the similarities she had observed between brother and sister were quite so superficial after all. Renata, she discovered, could be quite as ruthlessly single-minded as her older brother when she chose, and she was equally determined to have her way.

'Try them on!' she insisted for the umpteenth time, thrusting an armful of exquisite creations into Tanya's reluctant arms. Tanya had glimpsed the labels that they bore—names like Armani, Valentino and Ferre—and she shuddered to think what they must cost. But there was no getting out of it, she decided with a woeful shrug, and disappeared into the fitting-room to do as she was told.

Renata had chosen a cerise silk sheath for herself, strapless, and slit alluringly at one side from ankle to thigh. After a bit of bullying, Tanya plumped for a fairy-tale gown in pale, dull gold, full-skirted and narrow-bodiced with a flattering off-the-shoulder neckline. 'Wait till Fausto sees you in that!' Renata proclaimed with a wink as the assistant carefully folded it in layers of tissue paper in its box. 'He won't be able to take his eyes off you.'

Tanya bit her lip and glanced away as a barb of barren wretchedness tore at her like an iron claw. How little Renata understood of the crucial significance of the evening that lay ahead! To her it was just another party,

an excuse for dressing up and having fun. But Tanya
knew that tonight she would finally have to give Fausto
his answer—one way or the other. The deadline he had
set expired at midnight. And though her heart was
telling her she must say yes, her common sense
commanded otherwise. She was caught in a kind of
emotional deadlock from which she could see no escape.

Emma was waiting for them in the hall when they got
back. 'The *signor* wants you both to join him on the
terrace right away,' she informed them, her plump face
flushed with the excitement of the day. Then she leaned
towards Tanya with a confidential smile. '*Signorina*,
your father has arrived.'

With a squeal of delight, Tanya raced past her and
through the drawing-room to the terrace outside.
'Father!' She rushed towards him and threw herself
happily into his arms. But the smile on her face died
instantly as she caught sight of the blonde-haired
woman with the cat-like eyes who was seated, smug and
proprietorial, at Fausto's side.

CHAPTER NINE

'WHAT a clever girl you are!' The Countess Bea raised her wine glass to her shiny, coral-painted lips and smiled at Tanya condescendingly. 'Fausto took us to see the old wash-house while you were gone, and it really is quite extraordinary. Not at all in the style that I had expected, of course, but quite delightful all the same.' And she turned her blonde head to her host and smiled one of her dazzling smiles.

Fausto had been staring absently into his empty glass. He glanced up now and flicked some speck of imaginary dust from the immaculate sleeve of his light blue shirt. 'It's exactly as I wanted it,' he said. 'A first-class job.'

'I think it's beautiful. I'm very proud of you.' Devlin clasped his daughter's hand and Tanya turned again to look at him. The dismay she had felt on discovering that the countess had arrived in advance for the party and would be staying at the villa overnight had been largely tempered by immense relief the moment she had looked into her father's face. He was a man transformed. Since she had seen him last, just over two weeks ago, he had shed ten years. The blue eyes were sparkling with humour and vitality and the hard, grey lines of weariness had vanished from his face. His very bearing and manner of speech told of a rediscovered dynamism and love of life.

Tanya smiled wryly to herself, knowing to whom it was that she owed thanks for that. In spite of the upheaval he had wrought in her own life, she was only too sharply aware that it was Fausto's intervention that had saved her father's life. It was many, many months

161

since she had seen Devlin looking as ebullient and fit as he was looking now. And she felt a tiny stab of guilt, remembering some of the harsh, ungrateful accusations she had hurled at Fausto in the past, though her guilt was eased by jealous anger now as she frowned across the table at him. Why hadn't he told her the countess was coming? And why was it necessary for her to be here quite so early anyway? For what reason did she, out of all the scores of guests invited, have to stay at the villa overnight? And above all, she found herself wondering with increasing ire, why did the ridiculous woman have to be sitting quite so close to him?

If Fausto was in the least aware of the stream of angry questions that were buzzing through her head, he certainly gave no outward sign of it. He seemed vaguely distracted, in spite of an outward show of conviviality, as though his deeper thoughts were occupied elsewhere. What was he thinking of? she asked herself, her eyes taking in the strong, dark profile in a single glance. He looked, as usual, so utterly and unshakeably self-possessed. Could he possibly be thinking of her, wondering what her answer to his proposal of marriage was going to be? Somehow she doubted it. He was probably just quietly savouring the prospect of sharing his bed with the countess tonight.

The countess, for her part, was doing her best to fire such thoughts. The silky, coral-coloured top she was wearing clung to her body like a second skin, the deep V at the front revealing an ample cleavage. And as she talked, her coral-tipped fingers constantly toyed with the thin gold chains she wore around her neck, blatantly inviting the inscrutable dark eyes to wander downwards to her breasts. From time to time, as she made some point, her hand would reach out to rest lightly on his sun-bronzed arm. That Fausto and she were lovers was clearly something she was quite happy for the table at large to know.

Tanya seethed inwardly, fighting to keep the hurt she felt from showing in her face. Once, it had taken Fausto's taunting accusation to force her to recognise the cruel emotion burning inside her for what it really was. By now it had become uncomfortably familiar—the humiliating lash of jealousy.

She almost didn't notice that he was watching her. As their eyes met, he smiled, an odd smile, then abruptly he shifted his gaze to Devlin, consulting his watch. 'I think now would be as good a time as any,' he said, 'for us to have our little talk.'

The older man nodded and rose to his feet. 'I'll see you later, Tanya,' he said as Fausto abruptly pushed back his chair and took his leave of the assembled company. 'Signor Cabrini and I have a couple of matters to discuss.'

After the two men had gone, the women continued to sit around the table for a while. The countess poured herself another glass of wine and leaned back in her seat with a self-satisfied sigh. The brightly painted lips curved into a catlike smile. 'I hear you two went shopping this morning,' she purred, addressing herself to Renata. 'Did you manage to find something nice?'

The dark-haired woman raised one shapely eyebrow and returned the smile. Her expression, Tanya observed, was remarkably similar to the expression she had seen so many times on Fausto's face. A mixture of mild amusement and disdain. 'We think so,' she replied. 'But you can judge for yourself when you see us at the party tonight.'

The countess took a long sip of her drink and her gaze shifted to Tanya as she said, 'You must be very excited about tonight. I don't suppose you've ever been to a party quite like this before.'

Tanya bristled at the insult implicit in the remark, but before she could think of some suitable reply Renata cut in. 'We're all excited, aren't we? Fausto's little dos are always fun. And I can tell you one thing,' she added with an elegantly provocative smile. 'This young lady here is going to be the belle of the ball. In the dress she'll be wearing, there won't be another woman present who can hold a candle to her.'

A faint flush of colour crept into Tanya's cheeks. Renata was overdoing it a bit. But her barbed remark had unquestionably found its mark. The countess winced and smiled a smile that somehow never reached her eyes.

With graceful composure, Renata rose from her seat. 'I think I'll go and have a little siesta now,' she said. 'I'm quite tired out.'

'Me, too.' Tanya stood up hurriedly, relieved at the opportunity to escape.

As they walked from the terrace and made their way through the drawing-room towards the hall, Renata touched Tanya lightly on the arm. 'I'm sorry,' she said, 'but the Countess Bea never fails to bring out the bitch in me. She really is an absolute——' She bit her lip and shuddered. 'And it's true, I really do need to lie down for a while after a solid hour of her company. She wears me out.'

Tanya laughed. 'I know exactly what you mean.'

As they parted company on the upstairs landing, Renata suddenly turned to her, a strangely searching expression on her face. 'Don't let that silly woman get to you,' she said. 'She just isn't worth it, I promise you.' Then added, with a meaningful smile, 'Believe me, you have nothing to worry about.'

What did she mean by that? Back in her room, Tanya stared at her reflection in the mirror and asked herself just how much Renata had guessed. Probably just about everything, she feared. There wasn't much that escaped those bright, intelligent dark eyes. And she herself, she knew, was not much good at camouflage. The powerful longing she felt for Fausto, the electric responses that rushed through her the moment he walked into a room, the way her heart leapt every time he looked at her, must be blatantly obvious to all but the most dim-sighted observer. So the rampant jealousy that inevitably seemed to afflict her whenever the countess was around must be blatantly obvious too. But why had Renata said that she had nothing to worry about?

She sank down on the bed and kicked off her sandals. Then, on an impulse, she pulled open the drawer of the bedside table and gazed down at the little leather-bound box that lay inside. Since Fausto had given her the ring, she had never looked at it again, had never even dared to open up the drawer in which it had lain till now.

Very gingerly, she picked it up and with trembling fingers raised the lid. The big solitaire diamond flashed at her as though illuminated by a thousand lights, and she almost gasped out loud at its magnificence. She shook her head and smiled to herself. Trust Fausto to be extravagant! Then, with a delicacy bordering almost on reverence, she lifted the ring slowly from its satin bed. It was beautiful, more beautiful than anything that she had ever owned, and it had been given to her by the only man she had ever wanted in her life.

Involuntary tears sprang to her eyes. Fausto had said that she must keep it whether she accepted his proposal of marriage or not, but she had always known that she could not do that. If she left, then she would leave the ring behind—for if she turned him down she also knew that she would have to go. At once. There could be no alternative. And he would not try to stop her. She knew him well enough to understand that now. A wrench of pain tore at her heart to think that if she left this place she would probably never see Fausto again.

She jammed the ring back in its box and snapped the lid shut. Could she really live with that? Never to see his face again, to feel his arms around her or taste the sweetness of his lips on hers? Never again to hear his voice or thrill to the warmth of his body against hers? Never again to see him smile? Her fingers tightened round the little box as she clutched it, trembling, to her heart. She could not, any more than she could take a life, sentence herself to the wretched existence that her own life would surely be if he was not a part of it.

Yet the fear in her lingered as she laid the box back in the drawer and pushed it shut. How could she lay her heart and soul at the mercy of a man who took pride in claiming that he had neither heart nor soul himself? A man who treated women like playthings? A man she wasn't even sure that she could trust?

But why had Renata told her that she had nothing to worry about?

Too many questions. She closed her mind and took refuge in a long, hot, soothing bubble-bath. Just as she was drying herself, the blue phone rang. It was Devlin.

'I'm sorry I took so long to get back to you, sweetheart,' he apologised, 'but Fausto and I got chatting and——' He laughed. 'Well, you know how it is with us businessmen.'

Tanya couldn't suppress a grin. It was heart-warming to hear her father laughing and making jokes again. It had been so long. It was also warming to hear that he and Fausto were on first-name terms at last. 'That's all right,' she assured him. 'As a matter of fact, I've just been having a nice long bath.' And trying to make some pretty important decisions about my life, she added wryly to herself. But that was something, for the moment, she preferred her father not to know.

'Listen, Tanya,' he continued, 'once you're dressed,

why not drop round to my room for a drink? We can have half an hour on our own together before the party starts.'

'I'd like that,' she agreed. She hadn't had a chance for a proper chat with her father since he had arrived. 'I'll be with you in about an hour.'

Fausto had said the guests would probably start arriving about eight. It was now just after six, so she had plenty of time. Not that she had the least intention of rushing anyway. Renata's generous prediction that she was destined to be the belle of the ball might have been slightly over the top considering the elegant company she would be mingling with tonight, but at least she was determined she was going to look her very best. Tonight, after all, could prove to be one of the most important nights of her entire life, one way or the other.

She sat down at the dressing-table to apply her make-up, suddenly grateful that she was going to spend some time with her father before joining the party. Half an hour with him, she hoped, might help to soothe her troubled mind, might even give her the courage to make her choice once and for all.

Even for such a grand occasion, she decided, her lightly tanned complexion required little make-up. A touch more mascara than usual, perhaps, and a smudge of colour on her upper lids to emphasise her tawny eyes. She brushed her lips with a soft rose lipgloss and swept her hair up into a golden coil high on her head, anchoring it securely with the two gilt butterfly pins she had bought in Milan. Then she sprayed her pulse points liberally with scent. Now for the dress.

It felt like stepping into a dream, she thought as she adjusted the voluminous skirts and fastened the row of tiny hooks that formed an invisible fastening at one side. The sweeping neckline revealed no more than the soft upper curve of the full swell of breasts and showed off the fine lines of her shapely shoulders to perfection. The dull gold colour, just a shade or two lighter than her hair, was subtly flattering, the sheen of the silk reflecting a warm glow to her skin. As she slipped on the gold kid sandals that Renata had insisted she buy as well, she felt grateful that she had taken the older woman's advice. Though she said it herself, she had never looked better in her life.

Her steps were light as she hurried down the corridor to her father's room and she almost didn't notice the blonde-haired figure poised for descent at the top of the stairs. The countess's dress—what little there was of it—was a brightly coloured, sequin-encrusted concoction in shades of lime-green and mauve, and thick bands of diamonds and emeralds blazed at her wrists. She looks like the Blackpool illuminations, Tanya told herself dismissively, determinedly remembering what Renata had said: 'Don't let that silly woman get to you . . . You have nothing to worry about.' Perhaps Renata knew something that Tanya did not.

Devlin's face lit up with pride the moment she walked into the room. 'You're a vision to behold,' he murmured, kissing her warmly on the cheek. 'If only your mother could see you now.'

She smiled. 'You're looking pretty dapper yourself.' And he was. The dark evening-suit and the head of neatly trimmed grey hair lent him a distinguished look, reminiscent, she thought, of the man he had been in former years. Perhaps, at last, the pendulum of fortune had begun to swing his way. The dark days over, a bright new future filled with hope spread out ahead.

She sat on one of the silk-upholstered bedroom chairs as he mixed her a martini from the tray of drinks that Emma had thoughtfully provided, and began to recount his activities of the past two weeks. He had been incredibly busy, re-establishing his old vital network of contacts in the art business, recruiting new and potential customers and making a not inconsiderable little profit for himself along the way.

'I know you've been through a lot of anxiety on my behalf,' he told her with a wry twist to his mouth, leaning towards her in his chair. 'But you really needn't worry any more. I hope you're finally convinced of that.'

She nodded, knowing that at last she really was.

'I even managed to convince Fausto this afternoon,' he continued, smiling. 'And he's a hard man to convince. He virtually threatened to have me locked up unless I promised not to overtax myself.'

Tanya smiled, knowing that Fausto was perfectly capable of carrying out his threat.

'But I managed to convince him there's no danger of that. I've been too close to the brink ever to risk it again.' Devlin leaned back in his seat and ran one finger contemplatively around the rim of his whisky glass. 'All the same, if things keep going the way they're going now, I should have my financial obligations to him cleared up in no time at all.'

'I know you'll do it, Father. I have every confidence in you.'

He nodded. 'Yes.' Then paused. 'Now what about you, young lady? I may be mistaken, but this afternoon I couldn't help feeling that you had something on your mind. Am I right?' He raised one eyebrow questioningly at her.

So Renata had not been the only one with sharp eyes, Tanya thought, meeting her father's quizzical gaze with a rueful shrug. 'Now don't you start worrying about me,' she admonished him cheerfully. 'I'm fine.'

'I always worry about you, my dear,' he started on a serious note. But before he could go on, a sharp tap on the bedroom door interrupted him. 'Come in!'

The door opened and Tanya's breath caught in her

throat as Fausto walked into the room. In the immaculately cut dinner-suit with its shiny silk lapels, the crisp white shirt and black bow-tie he looked like some dark prince from a fairy-tale come to carry her away. And she felt the blood rush through her veins and an almost intolerable longing for him clutch at her heart as he paused to gaze at her with those deep, dark eyes. 'You're looking very beautiful tonight,' he said.

'Thank you,' she heard herself murmur back self-consciously, hot colour flooding in her cheeks as she hastily clasped her hands together in her lap, hoping for some illogical reason that he hadn't noticed the absence of the ring.

But he had turned to Devlin. 'I'm sorry to interrupt,' he said with a quick smile of apology. 'But, as promised, I've come to bring you this.'

It was only then that Tanya noticed what he was holding in his hand. The little fake icon that was indirectly responsible for everything that was happening to her. And her heart contracted with gratitude to him as she saw the look of pleasure on her father's face.

'When you first gave me this,' Fausto was saying, 'I believed its value to be in the order of several thousand pounds.' He smiled a mildly self-deprecatory smile. 'Now, of course, I realise that as a piece of art it is worth nothing—yet of a value beyond estimation in terms of what it means to you. I feel honoured that you trusted me enough to let it pass into my hands, and it is now my pleasure to return it to you.' He paused. 'I think we no longer have need of tokens and pledges——' and glanced quickly at Tanya before finishing '—of any kind.'

Nervously she looked away. So he was formally releasing her, granting her the absolute freedom to leave if she wished. Once, nothing would have pleased her more, but now the gesture sent a faint chill through her heart. She glanced back to find the dark gaze still fixed firmly on her face. Searching, it seemed, for some answer to the question in his eyes. Then he turned away abruptly and headed for the door. 'I'll leave you now. I have to see to my guests.'

Devlin had accepted the return of the icon without a word and stood gazing down at it, tears in his eyes. 'We'll be down in a couple of minutes,' he assured Fausto now. 'And thank you,' he added quickly, unable to disguise the thickening of emotion in his voice.

The tall, handsome figure paused in the doorway for a moment and the dark eyes locked with Tanya's as he spoke. 'I'll be waiting for you,' he said.

With the excuse that she had to fix her hair, Tanya persuaded her father to go downstairs to join the party ahead of her. Then she raced back along the corridor to her own room, her heart fluttering like a nervous bird. Suddenly she had no more doubts about what her decision must be. She loved him. It was as simple as that. And she had to be with him. Whatever the risks.

The ring felt cool and heavy as she slipped it on to the third finger of her left hand, noticing how perfectly it fitted her. A tremor of anticipation rippled through her as she tried to imagine the expression on Fausto's face when he saw that she was wearing it. Whatever his reasons were for asking her to marry him, she vowed, she would make him love her, even if it took her the rest of her life. No longer would she be afraid of what she felt for him. It might continue to tear her apart at times— but, given the choice, she would learn to live with that.

A surprising number of guests had already arrived, filling the spacious drawing-room with laughter and bright party talk, spilling out on to the terrace, illuminated now, like the gardens below, by thousands of tiny, hidden lights. A five-piece dance combo played discreetly in one corner and one or two couples had already taken to the floor. She glimpsed her father standing in a group with the Banuccis, the couple she had dined with that first evening in Milan. Gabriella Banucci waved and smiled as she caught sight of her, and Tanya made a gesture to indicate that she would join them later. First, she had to find Fausto. But there was no sign of him.

Her eyes searched impatiently through the crowd of unknown faces as she dodged past waiters carrying trays of food and drink. Where could he be? She frowned, aware of the unfamiliar weight of the ring on her finger and the sudden sharp tug of anxiety in her breast. Where had he gone? Why wasn't he here waiting for her as he had promised?

'Tanya!'

She whirled round to find Renata standing next to her, looking splendid in her cerise silk dress. 'Do you know where Fausto is?' Tanya demanded at once, not caring at the abruptness of her question nor the look of mild surprise it had brought to the older woman's face.

'I think he's in the library,' Renata answered, a watchful expression in the bright, dark eyes. 'But, Tanya, I——' She reached out a hand as though to stop the younger girl, but Tanya was already darting across the room, out into the hall and down the narrow corridor that led to the library at the other side of the house, running as though her feet had wings.

Her cheeks were flushed as she reached the door, and she paused for a moment to catch her breath, excitement pulsing through her like a charge of electricity. This was it. On a wave of tumultuous exhilaration, she pushed open the door.

The sight that met her eyes made her stiffen with horror and disbelief. Fausto was standing by the big leather couch at the far end of the room, his back to her. Not that he would have been likely to notice her even if he had been facing the door, she thought with sudden, bitter nausea. All his attention seemed to be focused on the half-sitting, half-reclining figure on the couch, whose emerald-clad arms were tightly wrapped around his neck. One strap of the countess's green and mauve dress had slipped from her shoulder, exposing a large expanse of naked breast and the strappy green sandals she had been wearing were kicked half-way across the library floor.

A stifled cry of pain tore from Tanya's lips as she stood in the doorway, paralysed. The dark head jerked round then to look at her and she saw anger flashing in the dark eyes. 'Tanya!' And he straightened abruptly and turned to face her, his features set in hard, tight lines. 'What are you doing here?'

Without a word, she ripped the ring from her finger with a trembling hand and flung it at him across the room. Then she stumbled back outside into the corridor, ashen-faced, on legs almost too numb to carry her.

'Tanya, come back!'

She heard his call, but she was already half-way to the hall, running on swift, stiff legs, desperately fighting back the tears that almost blinded her.

In the hallway she paused, a sudden panic clutching at her throat. She had to get out of here, out of this house, away from him, as far as possible. If she went to her room, there was a possibility that he might follow her there, and she knew she could not bear to face him now, could not bear to listen to the stream of silken lies that would surely issue from his lips, nor endure the cruel indifference that she would see in the dark eyes.

On an impulse, she swung into the drawing-room, fighting to control her nerveless limbs as she battled her way through the thickening throng of party guests, the faces she pushed past a misty, indeterminate blur, the music and laughter that surrounded her no more than a dull throb in her ears. She reached the terrace and her pace quickened as she headed for the steps that led down into the garden. Then she was running, her long skirts billowing out behind her like a spinnaker in the wind and her gold hair tumbling down around her shoulders as she headed instinctively for the narrow, flag-stoned path that led away between the trees at the foot of the lawn.

Only the pale light of the moon illuminated her way as she stumbled onwards through the silent wood, the only sound the painful sobbing of her breath, her only sensation the sharp ache that had descended like an icy shroud around her heart.

At last, she emerged into the little clearing where the old wash-house stood. Here she would be safe. He would not find her here. And she almost collapsed through the front door, falling against it as she slammed it shut and with quivering fingers snapped the lock. Her face was wet with tears as she sank, trembling, exhausted, to the floor, her body wrenched with an agony of bleak despair as she fought to banish from her mind the cruel vision of the scene she had witnessed in the library.

But it was etched in fire across her brain. Fausto, the man to whom she had been on the brink of offering her very soul, locked in the semi-naked embrace of the woman he had flaunted in her face right from the start. And she shivered as she saw again the flame of anger in his eyes when he had turned to find her watching them. Nothing could ever wash that memory away, no bland excuses ever dull the savage treachery of his cruel-hearted faithlessness.

She started at the sudden sound of footsteps approaching the door and shrank back as an unknown hand wrestled with the doorknob.

'Go away,' she whispered beneath her breath. 'Leave me alone, whoever you are.'

Impatient knuckles rapped against the door. 'I know

you're in there, Tanya. Open up.'

Renata's voice. She held her breath.

'Open the door, Tanya, do you hear? I'm not moving from this spot until you do.'

'Leave me alone, Renata—please.' Her voice choked on a sob. Her knuckles clenched.

'Open the damned door, Tanya, or I'll get someone to come and break it down. I mean it. Open the door at once, I want to talk to you.'

Reluctantly Tanya staggered to her feet, wiping her damp face with the back of her hands. A note of deadly seriousness in the older woman's voice warned her it was no idle threat—and the last thing she felt able to cope with now was an ugly scene. Her fingers fumbled with the lock and the door pushed open as Renata strode inside, a grim expression on her face as she quickly snapped on the hallway light.

'Go through to the living-room,' Renata ordered, and instantly snapped on the light in there as well. Tanya obeyed, sinking into one of the chintz-covered arm-chairs with a defeated sigh.

Renata sat down opposite her and surveyed her with a calmly appraising eye. 'I knew this was going to happen,' she said. 'Fausto told me what a little hothead you are.'

A dull anger flared deep in the tawny eyes. 'Fausto!' she spat contemptuously, writing him off in a single, unforgiving breath.

Renata smiled, a humourless, ironic little smile. 'Yes, Fausto.' She sighed. 'I know all about what happened in the library. The minute I saw you rushing off down here I knew. But you happen to have got it all wrong, you know.'

'How could I? I saw the whole disgusting, sordid scene with my own eyes!'

'What you saw and what you thought you saw, in this

particular instance, Tanya, are not the same.' Renata sat back in her chair and crossed her long legs at the knees, an expression of divine oracle etched upon her lovely face. 'I'd be happy to tell you what was really going on, of course—if you want to know.'

Tanya stared at her dully. Renata was wasting her time. 'I know exactly what was going on. Your brother and the countess were making love.'

'Wrong.' Renata adjusted the cerise silk of her dress over her knees. 'That is what you thought was going on. My brother was not making love to the countess. Far from it. In fact, I'm sure there was nothing further from his mind. Semi-conscious, drunken women, I'm sure, are not what turn my brother on.'

A spark of interest was starting to dawn in Tanya's eyes. 'So what are you trying to tell me, then?' she asked.

'If you'll listen, I'll explain.' Renata could sense her growing impatience, but she took her time. 'As you may have noticed earlier this afternoon, our dear friend the countess has been imbibing pretty heavily all day. By the time she got down to the party, she was already pretty drunk—and, I can assure you, Fausto was not amused. I was with him, helping him to greet the guests as they arrived, and he was getting angrier by the minute, especially when she started drawing attention to herself.'

She paused to ensure that she still had Tanya's undivided attention before going on. 'It must have been just about ten minutes or so before you arrived on the scene that the wretched woman passed out cold. I suggested to Fausto that he carry her through to the library and stretch her out on the sofa for a while. Which he did—and that, of course, was where you came in.' She made a little grimace. 'I tried to stop you going after them, but you were too quick for me. I guessed you'd jump to the wrong conclusion—and I was right, of course.'

Tanya's eyes had never left Renata's face. She was stunned into silence, numbed by the grossness of the error she had made. But, at last, she found her voice. 'It doesn't make any difference,' she said. 'She's still his mistress, after all.'

'What nonsense!' Renata laughed. She seemed to find the accusation genuinely comical. 'Fausto's no angel, I admit, but credit him with a little more taste and refinement than that! Oh, I know the way she throws herself at him, and it annoys me too. She's been trying to get her clutches into Fausto ever since her husband died.' She sighed. 'Fausto puts up with her because her late husband was a very close friend—and because he promised the count before he died that he'd keep an eye on his widow and her financial affairs. But there's nothing going on between the two of them—as I already tried to tell you this afternoon. I'd stake my very last dollar on it.'

More than anything, Tanya wanted to believe. But she had to be sure. 'That's certainly not the impression he's given me. I even asked him once. He didn't deny that it was true.'

'He didn't actually confirm it, though?'

'No.'

'Hah! Men!' Renata scoffed and made a `face. 'Probably he was just trying to make you jealous. Have you thought of that?'

'No.' It had never even crossed her mind. 'Why would he want to make me jealous anyway?'

'Because the man's in love with you! Why else?'

Hot colour flooded into Tanya's face. She could scarcely believe what she'd just heard. 'How do you know that he's in love with me?'

Renata shook her head indulgently. 'For one thing, it's written all over his face. And, for another——' she cupped her chin in the palm of her hand and smiled across at the younger girl '—he told me so himself.' The dark eyes gleamed. 'He also told me he was going to marry you. He even showed me the ring he'd bought while he was over in New York.'

To Tanya it felt as though an enormous load had suddenly been lifted from her back—only to be replaced by another, even heavier one. It looked as though she had been wrong about practically everything, misjudged him totally.

She listened with a sudden tight feeling in her chest as Renata went on, 'I was pleased. Pleased above all that it was you—and also that he'd finally decided to get hitched. We were all beginning to think he never would. He always said he never would. But that, I suppose, was understandable.' Her expression sobered suddenly. 'Fausto and I grew up, you see, in the sort of unhappy household that tends to make one lose faith in the sacred institution of matrimony. A battlefield more than a home.' She paused at Tanya's sympathetic nod. 'I see he's already mentioned this to you?'

'Briefly.'

Renata sighed. 'I think it affected Fausto more than it affected me. It certainly forced him to grow up very fast. Our father had very little time for us, you see, and from when he was comparatively young, it was Fausto, really, that our mother and I came to depend upon. He was very good to our mother. He worked harder than any son could reasonably be expected to to make up to her for the way our father treated her.' She smiled a fond smile. 'He's not the hard man he pretends to be, you know. Not deep down, anyway. He cares about people—and he's much more vulnerable and sensitive than he would like the world to think.'

So much for his claim that he possessed neither conscience, soul nor heart! But that was no help to Tanya now. She had behaved like a spoiled, impetuous and immature fool, all the things that he had accused her of. She felt an overwhelming sense of shame. Shame and deep, unbearable regret. 'I've ruined everything,' she said. 'I even threw his ring at him.'

'I know.' The dark-haired woman's face was serious again. 'And, as you've probably already guessed, he was absolutely furious.' Her eyes searched Tanya's almost anxiously. 'But you do love him, don't you?'

Tanya nodded and blinked as a hopeless tear slid slowly down her cheek. 'I do, with all my heart,' she vowed. Then she brushed the tear away impatiently. 'What can I do?' she pleaded. 'Will he ever forgive me now?'

'I'll go and speak to him.' Renata rose to her feet and smoothed the bright silk of her dress. 'I'll try to persuade him to come and talk to you.' Then she added, almost reluctantly, her dark brows knitting in a frown, 'I can't promise anything, of course. But I'll do my best.' And she kissed Tanya lightly on both cheeks. 'Keep your fingers crossed,' she said.

Tanya watched from the open doorway until Renata had disappeared from sight along the flag-stoned path that led through the wood to the garden and the house. In spite of the warm breeze that blew up from the lake, she shivered as a shaft of cold fear twisted at her heart.

'Oh, God,' she whispered to the night, 'please let him give me one more chance.'

CHAPTER TEN

AFTER Renata had gone, Tanya dashed upstairs to the bathroom and splashed her tear-stained face with cold water. Then she ran her fingers quickly through her tumbled hair to give it some kind of order. She didn't look too bad, considering, she decided, studying her reflection in the mirror with a frown. A bit puffy still about the eyes, the lines around her mouth a trifle drawn, but at least she looked presentable. She would be able to face him without feeling a total idiot. If he came. If Renata succeeded in persuading him.

She decided to wait up on the roof. The little wash-house drawing-room felt suddenly claustrophobic; she needed air. She leaned against the iron railing, feeling the warm breeze caress her face as she breathed in deeply and gazed out across the trees towards the lake.

Oh God, what an absolute mess she had made of everything! Just a matter of weeks ago, the only man that she would ever love had asked her, in all sincerity, to be his bride—and what had her reaction been? First, to tell him that she did not care for him, then to keep him dangling on a string and, finally, to throw the ring that he had given her back in his face. It made her shudder just to think of it. If he never wanted to set eyes on her again, she could scarcely blame him. It would kill her, of course, but no one would ever be able to say it was his fault.

Not that that was any comfort now. Nor was there any point in wishing that she had done things differently. What was done was done. She could only pray that the price to pay was not too harsh.

180

Renata had said he was in love with her. Let her not have destroyed that love, she begged silently. Let there still be enough left in his heart for him at least to take pity on her now. And come. She clung to the railing and closed her eyes. Oh, God, please let Renata have persuaded him to come and talk. That much, at least. For, if he did not, she knew with a cruel and bitter certainty that she was lost. And lost, too, her only hope of happiness for all eternity.

A faint rustling from the undergrowth below caused her to start, and her heart lurched crazily in her chest as a tall, dark figure in evening-dress strode from the shadows and out into the clearing below. It was Fausto. He had come. Relief swept through her. So there was hope, after all—though she could tell from his stiff, impatient gait that the agony that she had brought upon herself was not quite over yet.

She was half-way down the stairs to the hall when he burst through the front door, and she felt her breath catch in her throat as she registered the grim expression on his face. For a long moment, as she continued to hover half-way down the stairs, they confronted one another in total silence. Tanya's heart was hammering uncomfortably and her mouth had suddenly gone dry.

'You wanted to talk to me, I understand?' he said at last. There was a brittle, uncompromising edge to his voice.

It flashed through her mind that she could simply throw herself at his feet and beg for clemency. But such a display, she knew for sure, would only make him scorn her more. Anyway, it was impossible. Her legs were rooted to the spot. She had difficulty, even, in mobilising her vocal chords as she stuttered, 'Fausto, I—I—I wanted to apologise.' Every inch of her tormented body, it seemed, was trembling.

'Apologise?' he mocked, his lips twisting in a bitter smile. 'There's no need to apologise. You've made your position abundantly clear, and you're perfectly entitled to do that.'

So he was going to make it hard for her. She was suddenly glad that she had decided against grovelling. In his present mood, he would quite enjoy helping her to rub her own nose in the dirt. 'I didn't mean that. I meant that I shouldn't have done what I did.' He probably knew what she was trying to say, but, as he frowned, she stumbled on, 'The ring. I shouldn't have thrown it at you. I didn't mean to. I had been wearing it.'

The dark eyes stared at her, as hard as stones, and she felt her heart shrink almost to nothingness inside. The worst had happened. He had refused to accept her apology. But, before he could speak and put his refusal into words, she hurried to assure him, 'I was wrong—about everything. About the countess, in particular. Renata told me. I don't blame you for being angry. I've behaved abominably.' And she took a deep breath. 'It's only because I——' Love you, was what she had been about to say, but she stopped herself short. The total honesty of the words still frightened her.

He gave a sneering little laugh. 'Only because you what? Only because you enjoy behaving like a silly, spoiled child? Is that it, Tanya? Because that's exactly how you behaved tonight.'

'I know that—and I've apologised. What more do you want?' She straightened and glared at him, suddenly angry through her misery. 'It wasn't *all* my fault, you know. If you'd made it perfectly clear from the start that you and the countess weren't having an affair, probably none of this would have happened.'

He shook his head, but she thought there was a faint smile now around his lips. 'No, Tanya. Why should you care about Bea when you told me you don't love me anyway?'

She stared at the floor and bit her lip. 'Maybe I was

wrong about that as well.'

He came towards her and held out his hand, and this time there was no doubt about the smile. 'Let's go through to the drawing-room,' he said. 'We can't talk here.'

On shaky legs, she descended the stairs, and the clasp of his hand was cool and firm as he led her through into the drawing-room and sat down on the wide, chintz-covered sofa, looking up at her. 'What's the matter, are you afraid to sit next to me?' he teased, sensing her hesitation.

'Of course not.' But, in a way, she was. She had as good as told him that she loved him then—but he, so far, had said nothing similar to her. Almost gingerly, she seated herself on the chintz-covered cushion next to him.

'Tanya.' He swivelled round to look at her. 'Let's forget all about what happened earlier tonight. An unfortunate misunderstanding, that's all it was. Renata tells me she's already explained everything. But, you know'—he reached out and tilted her chin with his fingertips, his dark eyes searching as they gazed into her face—'you really must learn to trust me more. Didn't I tell you that you could trust me, right from the start?'

She nodded, suppressing a blush as she recalled the intimate circumstances in which he had entreated her, 'Trust me.' Just before the first time they'd made love. 'I remember,' she said.

He smiled. 'You know, I'm not the Don Juan that you seem to think I am. I don't have dozens of mistresses littered around the place. And, since that night that I proposed to you, there's been only one woman in my life.'

The touch of his hand was like fire against her skin, scorching a trail of almost unbearable sensitivity as she felt the back of his finger slide upwards to caress the side of her cheek. 'I believe you,' she said. And she closed her eyes as he smoothed the hair back from her face. 'But do you still love me?' she asked.

'Good God, what a question! Of course I still love you!' And she felt a shiver of excitement run down her spine as his hand slid round behind her hair to touch her nape. Gently he drew her closer to him, his lips softly brushing the sensitive corners of her mouth. 'My darling Tanya, I could never stop loving you.'

She clung to him with a sob as his arms folded round her, his breath warm and sweet against her hair. She had longed so desperately to hear these words, and to feel deep in her soul that they were true. 'Please tell me again,' she whispered breathlessly.

He drew back then to look at her, a fierce intensity that she had never seen before shining from the deep, dark eyes. 'I love you, Tanya. And I'll spend my whole life telling you, if that's what you want.' Then he hesitated as a sharp frown creased between the straight black brows. 'But surely you've known that all along?'

She shook her head. 'I didn't dare believe that it was true.'

A look of honest amazement crossed the handsome, dark-tanned face. 'But why else did you think I asked you to marry me, my love?' And his frown deepened slightly as he went on, 'I would never have made love to you if I hadn't been absolutely sure that I loved you and wanted to marry you.' He smiled. 'I thought you were the one with all the doubts.'

'I think they were fears more than doubts,' she answered, smiling back at him. 'But they're all gone now.'

'You're sure?'

'I'm sure.' And somehow she knew that she would never be afraid again.

He kissed her face. 'You told me you were wearing the

ring. Does that mean what I think it means?'

'Yes.' She nodded happily. A warm exquisite joy such as she had never known before lit up her heart as she gazed now into the face that she adored. 'I love you, Fausto, and I want to marry you.'

His eyes filled with an almost overpowering intensity of love. 'I'll make you happy, Tanya. I promise you.' And her eyes closed as his arms tightened around her and his lips pressed down on hers again, turning the blood to fire in her veins with the tender, demanding urgency of his kiss.

On a wave of emotion, she sank back against the cushions, succumbing with a little moan to the warm, excited pressure of his body against hers, sliding her hands beneath the fabric of his jacket to caress the powerful male contours of his shoulders and chest. She sighed and shivered as she felt him slip one hand beneath the silken bodice of her dress to cup her breast, sending a thrill of white-hot passion piercing through her loins as his fingers gently probed its aching peak.

'We've wasted enough time on misunderstandings,' he growled at her with a kiss, his breathing rough and ragged in his throat. 'I'm not going to wait for you any longer, Tanya. I want us to be married right away.' He raised his head to look at her, a faint smile playing on his lips. 'How does next week sound to you?'

She lifted one hand to touch his face, her whole being suddenly awash with love for him, and ran her fingers through his thick, dark hair. 'Next week sounds fine to me,' she smiled.

Fausto bent to kiss her nose. 'That's settled, then.' He gently kissed each eye in turn. 'But the honeymoon will have to wait,' he added with a teasing smile. 'Till September. My new personal assistant isn't able to start work till then.' Tanya blinked at him in dumb astonishment as he added, still smiling, 'In the meantime, you can save me the job of showing the temporary secretary the ropes. She'll be joining us on Monday.'

Tanya gasped. 'Why, you sneaky devil!' Then laughed. 'You certainly didn't waste much time in finding someone to replace me! What made you think you'd need to anyway?'

He threw her an unrepentant grin and ran his fingers down her cheek. 'I understand you better than you think, my dear. If you had turned me down, I knew for certain that you wouldn't stay. And if you said yes—as I've hoped and prayed you would—then, let's just say that I have other things in mind for you than office work.' And he smiled at the faint flush that rose immediately to her cheeks. 'Apart from my own, strictly personal plans for you—and these, I promise you, will take up a large part of your day—I also intend calling upon your professional services. A bit of redecorating at the villa, for one thing. It could use a slightly more feminine touch.' He smoothed her hair back from her brow and bent to kiss her softly on the lips. 'That is, as I've already said, if I ever get round to actually allowing you to get out of bed.'

She blushed again and poked him playfully in the ribs. 'Beast,' she murmured happily, embracing him.

He kissed her ear. 'Which reminds me—the job I want you to put at the top of your list is a nursery. I've a feeling it won't be long before we're needing one.' And he gently nipped her lobe between his teeth. 'You understand, of course, that having my children is all part of the deal?'

A strange sensation twisted low down in her gut. 'I can think of nothing I want more. Unless it's just to spend my life with you.'

He rose to his feet, taking both her hands in his, and drew her gently from her seat to stand in front of him. 'You gave me a few anxious moments, you know.' He looked down at her with a wry glint in his eye. 'Specifically that time we went to Lugano to see your father about the icon. Afterwards, I half expected you'd insist I let you go.'

Oddly enough, she remembered, it hadn't really crossed her mind. She had been falling in love with him even then, though she hadn't known. 'And what would you have done if I had?' she asked now, curious.

'Oh, I'd have let you go,' he answered, his expression serious. Then he added, to her almost tangible relief, 'But I wouldn't have allowed it to end there, you understand. Sooner or later, I'd have come after you.' And he drew her face close to his chest and held her tight. 'I'd waited far too long for you to come into my life just to stand meekly by and let you walk right out of it again.' Softly he kissed the top of her head. 'I love you, Tanya. You're all I ever wanted in my life.'

And you are more than I ever dared to dream that I might have, Tanya acknowledged silently to herself as she leaned her head in perfect happiness against his chest.

Fausto reached into his jacket pocket and pulled out the ring. 'I think you dropped this earlier,' he told her with a smile. And Tanya watched with beating heart as he slipped it carefully into place on her left hand. He kissed her cheek. 'And now, let's go back to the party for a while. We have a very important announcement to make.'

A deep contentment filled her soul as Fausto took her by the hand and led her out into the perfect, star-filled night. Here begins my happiness, she thought. My happiness for all my life.

Harlequin Presents

Coming Next Month

1103 MISTRESS OF PILLATORO Emma Darcy
Crushed by a broken love affair, Jessica welcomes Gideon Cavilha's offer to
research his father's historical theories. Once at Pillatoro, his magnificent
family estate, she feels strangely as if she belonged. But her one chance of
staying there depends on her telling a lie!

1104 SMOKE IN THE WIND Robyn Donald
Six years ago Ryan Fraine had taken over Venetia's life and shattered it. And he
had chosen her cousin instead. Now, though he still seems to want her, and
Venetia feels he's entitled to know his son, she's too proud to be second
choice....

1105 SUBSTITUTE LOVER Penny Jordan
Stephanie never told Gray Chalmers the truth about her marriage to his
cousin, Paul. And she's avoided the town where he and Paul ran a boatyard and
Paul accidentally died. Now Gray needs her help and she owes him so much.
Can she return and face the memories?

1106 OUT OF CONTROL Charlotte Lamb
Marooned in her fogbound cottage with a particularly infuriating man, Liza's
well-ordered emotions—scarred by an adolescent indiscretion—threaten to
break down. Yet she's determined to resist G. K. Gifford's dangerous attraction,
sure that, to him, it's all just a game....

1107 CLOSE COLLABORATION Leigh Michaels
Mallory's first meeting with sociologist C. Duncan Adams leaves little hope that
he'll help with her cherished project. The trouble starts immediately, long
before she finds out about the woman in his life, and he learns about the men
in hers....

1108 A PAINFUL LOVING Margaret Mayo
Everyone on the Greek island of Lakades thinks Aleko Tranakas is the perfect
antidote for a young widow's loneliness. Not Kara. She doesn't want an affair,
especially with a practiced womanizer whose seductive charms remind her of
her husband. She won't make that mistake again!

1109 ULTIMATUM Sally Wentworth
Powerboat racing is the strong passion of Reid Lomax's life. Casey's fear is
equally strong—that she'll lose her newlywed husband in an accident. So she
presents him with an ultimatum that she thinks he can't ignore....

1110 A MOMENT OF ANGER Patricia Wilson
Nick Orsiani is a man accustomed to getting what he wants, and what he wants
now is Rachel. Rachel, however, soon initiates a plan of her own—a dangerous,
winner-take-all contest!

Available in September wherever paperback books are sold, or through
Harlequin Reader Service:

In the U.S.
901 Fuhrmann Blvd.
P.O. Box 1397
Buffalo, N.Y. 14240-1397

In Canada
P.O. Box 603
Fort Erie, Ontario
L2A 5X3

Temptation™

TEMPTATION WILL BE EVEN HARDER TO RESIST...

In September, Temptation is presenting a sophisticated new face to the world. A fresh look that truly brings Harlequin's most intimate romances into focus.

What's more, all-time favorite authors Barbara Delinsky, Rita Clay Estrada, Jayne Ann Krentz and Vicki Lewis Thompson will join forces to help us celebrate. The result? A very special quartet of Temptations...

- **Four striking covers**
- **Four stellar authors**
- **Four sensual love stories**
- **Four variations on one spellbinding theme**

All in one great month! Give in to Temptation in September.

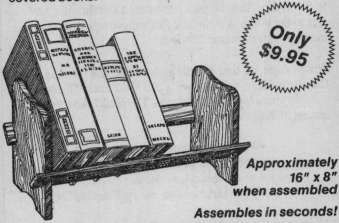